Dysphoria

an Appalachian gothic

by
Sheldon Lee Compton

Cowboy Jamboree Press
good grit lit.

First Edition
ISBN: 9781092736732

www.cowboyjamboreemagazine.com
www.bentcountry.blogspot.com

Cover and Interior Design: Adam Van Winkle
Cover Illustration: Adam Van Winkle

Cowboy Jamboree Press
good grit lit.

Praise for Sheldon Lee Compton

"Sheldon Lee Compton is the definition of what Faulkner meant when he described the closeness between the short story writer and the poet." - David Joy, author of The Weight of This World

"Sheldon Lee Compton is one of the new young breed of Kentucky writers–talented, fearless, and strong–bringing us word from the hills." - Chris Offutt, author of My Father the Pornographer

"A fierce and lyrical writer who, in his depiction of contemporary Appalachian life, is equal parts uncompromising and compassionate." - K. L. Cook, author of Love Songs for the Quarantined

"Sheldon Lee Compton is a hillbilly Bukowski, one of the grittiest writers to come down the pike since Larry Brown." - Donald Ray Pollock, author of Knockemstiff and The Devil All the Time

"Compton is an author whose art imitates life. A writer who understands the importance of portraying beauty and brutality in literature. A novelist who appreciates the elasticity of the defining line between right and wrong." - Matthew J. Hall in PANK

"Sheldon spins the hard and raw of his native soil into his characters, creating lives that are immediately poignant and real." - Kari Nguyen

"Sheldon Lee Compton is like a living, breathing John Cougar Mellencamp song (minus guitars and hand claps) but with much better stories." - Brian Alan Ellis, author of Something Good, Something Bad, Something Dirty

"Compton articulates the real hardscrabble world of contemporary Kentucky Appalachia he so intimately understands, writing with a stark and powerful but emotionally subtle voice." - Charles Dodd White, author of Sinners of Sanction County

"It's a damn hard world, but Compton still finds beauty and humanity in the hardness." - David S. Atkinson, author of Apocalypse All Time

"An Appalachian writer of consequence and influence." - April Bradley, editor at SmokeLong Quarterly

"We hear his characters in a way that brings them closer, that localizes them within our head, not just visually but audiovisually—it works to give each man, woman, child or teenager an incredibly substantive presence." - Michelle Bailat-Jones in Necessary Fiction

"No sooner had I read 'His hands were two leather balls folded in his lap,' the pool called 'Red Knife,' and Larry's back with its 'dinner-plate shoulder blades,' than I was hooked on Sheldon Lee Compton's Dysphoria: An Appalachian Gothic. The rhythms of its speech, word choices, depicted events, and sensory observations are a trip back home. The description of an old bedroom as having the 'scent of deep body odor' captures a memory of Appalachian lifestyle I know in my bones. Combined with the most believable characters and a harrowing plot, this is evocation of the heart's experience of Appalachia at its best." - Ron Houchin, author of The Man Who Saws Us in Half

"Dysphoria is ugly and gothic and morally questionable the way the best gothic writing should be, but then there's this innocence, these moments of tenderness and beauty, this intent to do good almost as much as bad. I think that's what makes me squirm the most. That these are real people, not headlines or punchlines. Often they are boys and men who can't fully escape being boys, but they've got real good and real bad in their heart, often doing the wrong thing in the name the right thing and vice versa. Time doesn't heal all wounds, it mostly makes them fester and boil over, the scab never fully crusting over. Time and Sheldon Lee Compton don't let anyone off easy, and that's just it, what makes Dysphoria timeless and never more relevant. It's that deadly mix of Old Testament

Vengeance, Original Sin, and Murphy's Law lurking around the corner of every action and reaction that makes you turn each page with one eye open and the other half-shut with a wince. And yet, with every page there's Compton, ever the wide-eyed witness to all of it, and not just them. Us too." -Benjamin Drevlow, author of <u>Bend with the Knees</u>

When a reader steps into the pages of a Compton story, the reader must maneuver through sharp edges, and wade in the mud of Sheldon's honest and poetic world in order to reach the reality of Sheldon's people, his characters. He's digging deep into the realness of his skin, a place most authors are scared to go to. <u>Dysphoria: An Appalachian Gothic</u> is Sheldon's masterpiece thus far. This book is like putting a revolver in to your mouth and pulling the trigger. Each bullet plugging the brain with honesty, pain, grit, fear, and truth. --Frank Reardon, author of <u>Interstate Chokehold</u>

In memory of my father, Orville Lee Compton

All I know is that I've wasted all these years looking for something, a sort of trophy I'd get only if I really, really did enough to deserve it. But I don't want it anymore, I want something else now, something warm and sheltering, something I can turn to, regardless of what I do, regardless of who I become. Something that will just be there, always, like tomorrow's sky.

— Kazuo Ishiguro,
When We Were Orphans

1

David Shannon gave his life savings to his son, Paul, on the third day of his funeral. It happened after most everyone left to get rest for the burial the next morning. Paul stayed, hands crossed in his lap, wondering why he hadn't cried yet. His mom wanted to be there for him, but wasn't sure her former in-laws would have cared for her attendance. Her uneasiness had infuriated Paul; his mom deserved to be anywhere she wanted at anytime she wanted. If ever a right had been earned, she had earned that one, at the very least. Returning to those thoughts was doing him no favors. He needed a restart. Clearing his mind, he sat in place for a long while, and did fairly well to find a calm center until the preacher dropped something beside him and clapped his shoulder as he passed.

Beside him in the church pew a folded flag lay orphaned. David had been a platoon sergeant in Vietnam and saved lives at some point forgotten in the family history. Or maybe saving lives became only part of the myth. Paul knew his father had been stationed in Korea for at least a year, away from the front lines, and that he led a platoon of men, but the soldiers he ordered were ordered to fix trucks more than kill anyone or save anyone. Sergeant David Shannon spent a lot of time overseeing a base garage. Paul knew this, but families sometimes liked to forget the mundane that actually happened in order to make a nice arrangement of false glory they wanted to remember.

The burial would be a long drawn out thing with twenty-one gun salutes and a presentation of the flag again and starched-stiff military uniforms filled out with an unknown handful of veterans who had served with his father and of whom very few would even so much as speak for more than ten seconds.

Paul wasn't alone in the church, though. His uncle Hillman stood in the sinner's foyer when Paul made it to the back doors. In the sinner's foyer were the restrooms and water fountain, along with a bulletin board with the phone numbers and addresses of church members who had moved away to other states. Some moved for work, others retired, and some had actually been ousted for any variety of transgressions reflecting poorly on the church family. Brother Ethan put their names up on the board, though, as if they had decided to stop attending. Paul wasn't sure if this was compassion or shame on the preacher's part. Hill sure didn't care.

The sinner's foyer is the place Hill could always be found during a funeral or a church service, his eyes low to the ground, feet pulled together like a scolded child. Paul respected him for being unpretentious, so when Hill stopped him in the foyer and shoved a Mason jar at him, Paul smiled and relaxed.

The jar showed three quarters full of faded and wrinkled dollar bills, tattered green rectangles like flags left from lost battles. Near the bottom rested sunken copper and silver. Loose change. Hill handed the jar over and didn't say anything. Instead, he pointed to a wad of yellow paper at the top of the jar. He tapped the side of the jar with a greasy fingernail and eased out the door to the porch. Paul could see Hill's black dress pants were too short. Probably bought them at the Goodwill yesterday. When he sat on the top steps of the porch, they became even shorter. Hill wore white athletic socks with wingtips. It was the first time he had seen Hill without boots on.

Paul sat beside Hill and his uncle moved his arms up and down his body like a game show host showing off a new sports car and said, "Don't I clean up pretty?"

"Everything but that face," Paul said.

Hill laughed, patted Paul on the shoulder, and stood up. "Come over before you head back. Your mom doing okay?"

"Okay, Uncle Hill," Paul said. "Yeah Mom's okay. You know her. She takes it on the chin."

"Hell yeah she does," Hill said and lumbered down the front steps with a wounded fluttering of loose shirt, piled into his S-10 pickup, and mufflered away.

Paul knew the wad of yellow paper was a letter, but he didn't read it at the church. When he made it to his grandparents' house, he slinked into the back bedroom. In the bedroom were stacks of books and magazines, pill bottles and various toys saved over the years from when Paul was young. Pictures of Paul were turned backwards on small tacks punched into the walls. Two on the wall to the left of his father's old bed and one above a shelf filled with what-nots. His face smiled in those pictures, though no one could see him. One of him on Christmas Eve wearing a new Chicago Bears jersey. His father lurked behind him, slumped onto the couch and glaring at the camera — hateful, harried, ready for a finish to the holiday. The other two were of Paul alone. School pictures. Smiling because he was at school and away from home. The pictures were turned backwards because his father said it was unbearable to see him and know how he had failed as a father, and he couldn't take them down because they were pictures of his son.

Taking the pictures off the wall, Paul noticed how the room captured the scent of deep body odor. He sat on the bed and read the first sentence of the letter.

I'm sorry.

Then he read it out loud, and let out a breath like he wanted to spit the words back out before they passed by his heart.

2

The kitchen. Warm brown colors. The scent of hot cornbread, butter, fried pork, and soup beans wrapped everything in a sort of a good haze. Beneath that, and hardly detectable, existed the knife-edged presence of February cold. A strong wind came in from under the kitchen door, but went unnoticed in the warmth still coming off the stove near the dining table. Paul slid a fork across his dinner plate. It was a sound he barely noticed, concentrating on each bite.

Paul's grandmother sat at the head of the table and his father sat across from him, busy with his own plate of food. He absently poked his fork into a mound of mashed potatoes. Paul didn't look up from his plate, didn't notice how his father stared at him.

Blank.

Nothing.

Two tired blue eyes gazing out at some lost point behind Paul, beyond the kitchen. Staring into some forever hell, mute to everyone else, nothing more than the lull sounds of the winter wind beneath the door to his ear, but growing every time Paul pulled the fork across the plate. His mouth pulled into a long and permanent frown so the corners of his horse-hair mustache rubbed close to the exact middle of his chin.

The mouth was one hard part of a face stripped of emotion and pock-marked from severe acne.

Paul's grandmother said not a word in her chair, but her eyes cruised the space around her, moved slowly in the sockets, expectant.

Paul saw only his own hands. He kept his head down and there were only the screeches and pulls. He loved mashed potatoes. It seemed no one ever bragged about mashed potatoes, he thought, and this was sad. It was always something about the pork chops being good and tender or how the cornbread and the butter just melted into each other. Good cornbread and pork chops. But there were mashed potatoes, too, and no one ever said anything about them. People just shoveled them in, and most of the time they left a lot behind, not caring, moving on to have coffee or smoke cigarettes or watch *Sanford & Son* before bed. Paul loved them, though, and they were gone after this serving. He had already eyed the cooker and knew they were gone. Everybody had just enough, but he wanted more. So he pulled his fork slowly, trying to get the last bit of them along the edge of the plate.

Then the room exploded and everything brightened with a blue electricity.

Paul's father jumped out of his chair. His grandmother leaned back, surprised, and flung her arms out to either protect herself or stop her son, or both somehow. She whimpered out a quiet and pitiful sound and moved until her back was against the refrigerator.

Fierce blue eyes and tangled '
shook across the room. It seemed the
wind blew in from behind him so that he
toward anything else at all, just away from co
pain and away from it like a bullet warmed from a
barrel, and that fast. His fast moving mouth and
ragged yelling became the sensory world. His stomach
walls beat ancient rhythms against his ribs—flee, flee,
flee. His fork fell to the floor.

Paul rushed past his father, who grabbed the
sides of the table and gained ground across the kitchen.
He struggled around a corner and into the hallway, but
fell roughly on the hole in the carpet that had been
there since before he was born and tore raw streaks
across his knees. The pink burns immediately ached
through to his kneecaps, but behind him the sound of
heavy breathing continued and so he pin-balled his
way through the hallway. The breathing coming from
behind him interrupted shouted questions about what
he thought he was doing. Was he starved to death?
Wasn't there enough food? Was he so hungry he had to
scrape the plate over and over and over?

Flee, flee, flee.

The entire thing happened fast, and, years later,
Paul would shorten his memory of it even more,
through effort forget most of it except the last, when it
had almost ended and he was in the bed, under the
covers, watching with a concentration and a love like
prayer. He would only remember because he couldn't
forget when his father cornered him in the bathroom,

t low into his face where he had stuck himself
etween the bathtub and the clothes hamper and
screamed at him in a blur of anger and sickness, manic
and out of control, without regret until too late, when it
no longer mattered.

3

Paul looked out the dirty cab window and thought about his father dressed up in clown makeup. It wasn't really a cab. A cab was a cab. This was a Ford Taurus some guy bought along with about three other of the same make and model and had painted before slapping magnetic Big Sandy Transport signs on the doors. This guy, who made his living having employees drive old people and people drawing disability or social security from small towns in eastern Kentucky to places like Lexington and Louisville for doctor appointments, wouldn't know what it meant to *keep it running* to save his life.

So here he was, Paul thought, looking out a smeared window of a not-cab leaving again a family he hadn't seen in years. His grandparents were the only ones he really cared about anymore. Uncle Hill could come and go in a person's life without changing much one way or another, if he chose for that to be the case. He moved like an iceberg among other people, hiding himself mostly beneath the water, never having to get too close because, like icebergs, people navigated around Uncle Hill. Family behind him, a city full of people lacking the heart and guts of his childhood in front of him, and here Paul was in his not-cab wishing now he'd driven in a rental.

He never drove himself anymore. He became adjusted to life in a city where people bought vehicles mostly to announce their financial arrival. Transportation was a bonus. He paid thousands of dollars over the years waving real cabs and tipping drivers. Never thought he'd find himself in a state of mind where he'd spend money to have people drive him places and not own a car himself. But that's just what he did. Philadelphia wasn't by a stretch New York or Los Angeles, but it was the biggest place Paul had ever been and the biggest place he'd likely ever live. It was big enough for him. Big as three worlds when he first moved there, and the same now. Back in Kentucky, just forty miles from the town he grew up in, coming back from seeing his father lying dead with makeup on in a casket that cost more than every stitch of clothes his father had bought in the last ten years total, Paul was taking a not-cab because he did not own a vehicle. That kind of detail would get him certified insane in Red Knife.

He had worn his gray suit on the ride in and wore it again now heading back to the airport in Lexington. It was his best suit. Now he regretted that decision, too. In the backseat with him sat a withdrawn older man. Paul hadn't asked, but he knew multiple passengers was a common thing for this transportation service. So many people traveled to Lexington for doctor appointments, they really had no choice. County budgets only went so far.

The man had on seersucker pants, the kind painters sometimes wore, and a faded denim shirt. His silhouette from the light coming in the car window was stronger somehow than his face in full sunlight might have been, tough from years of labor. With the shadows working his profile, Paul could see from where he sat the deep grooves of wrinkles trenching the skin across the high points of the man's cheekbones. He did not have the look of a man who owned many suits. His hands were two balls of leather folded in his lap.

Paul turned his attention out his window and tried not to stare. It was a habit he picked up. Not noticing. He wanted to tell the man he only owned one other suit, a black one, and that he couldn't afford to even fill out his work wardrobe enough to pay for the blue suit for a three-color spread. He wanted to tell him he barely had the money to fly back from the funeral, that he nearly had to hitchhike to the Mountain Parkway and hope in the past fifteen years a bus had started a route from Salyersville to Lexington, but since the driver had stopped near a railroad crossing to wait on the man to make his way up a hill from a small walking bridge where he had been waiting, the man had said nothing. The driver asked if he was going to the UK Clinic when he got in, the man had nodded, and it had been silence since. It had moved beyond feeling awkward in the car. For the past thirty minutes, Paul and the older man had mostly stared out their smeared windows and the hills on each side of them.

When they were roughly ten minutes or so from UK Clinic, the man glanced across the seat between them and sniffed the air. Paul wore a seventy-dollar splash of cologne. He bought it four years ago and still hadn't taken the neck out of it, wearing it less than a half dozen times, including this morning. The old man smelled like wood heated by summer sun mixed with hand-washed clothes and leather and dried tobacco. He couldn't know how much Paul actually appreciated him after seeing men walking metrosexually from one block to the next in the city for so many years. Others he had seen dressed in designer work shirts, wearing two-hundred dollar Timberland work boots, striving to grow full beards to seem as much of a man as they could, hoping to carry and exude some Hollywood idea of hard work and a tough life.

About ten minutes after he sniffed the air between them, the man turned around in his seat. He was small with soft blue eyes and hair combed back from his forehead. Sunlight highlighted the stubble that had taken over his face. He cleared his throat.

"You ever wonder what this place looked like before they settled in?" he asked. His voice was soft but cracked between syllables as if he might have only talked when needed. "I mean before the trail blazers came through and built the places and put people around."

Paul nodded and tried on an easy smile. He expected the old man, though sufficiently a hard-earned survivor of his environment and worth that honor, to eventually offer some rhetorical pleasantry and Paul had perfected the ability to show just enough interest on the job. Offer a little smile. Not much, just a little from the corners of the mouth.

"It's funny, I guess," the man continued. "Some places just get settled and then some don't. Take the North Pole. That Byrd feller went all the way up there and jabbed our American flag, bless its soul, into snow and ice. But it ain't settled. Can't be. A place that cold and that far away from people. Way I figure it, that old Byrd was just running away. Run so far he made it to the top of the world, maybe. But all the same, he was just running." He leaned across the seat. "You running *from* something or running *to* something, young man?"

Hearing the man's voice surprised Paul and instead of replying, he only stared at him and studied him while the not-cab pulled under the front portico at the UK Clinic.

"Name's John Harper," the old man said. "Looks like you must've lived back there in Red Knife. Probably came in to see family, I guess. You have a nice day and a good trip back to wherever. It's good weather for traveling. Well, this is my stop. Nice talking to you."

Paul still didn't say anything. The man ease himself up and out of the vehicle and move gingerly through the sliding doors, watching them retract like spiders across one big web. Paul started to ask the driver to park so he could step in to grab a sandwich from the cafeteria and saw the old man turn around in the hospital foyer. He made his way back to where they sat idling under the portico. He held up his hand and, raising his voice above noise from New Circle Drive, said, "I'm sorry to hear about your father! Truth is, he died a long time ago. Just ask your uncle! Just ask your Uncle Hill!"

What? What had the old man just said? Paul touched the driver on the shoulder and stepped out, made a quick spin around the back of the Taurus, and ran for the sliding doors of the front entrance. The doors closed, paused in place while he stood there tapping his thighs, and then finally slid back open. The man was gone.

"I don't care if you want to pay me to take you back, buddy. You're acting like it's a big deal for some reason, and I was going to be driving straight back as soon as I dropped you at the airport anyways. What's the big deal? Geez. It's one-fifty to ride back, just like it was one-fifty to ride here with me."

The not-cab driver stood beside the Taurus smoking a cigarette. He wiped potato chip grease on his black sweatpants and checked a flip-phone every few seconds. He could care less, this driver, Paul thought. He didn't care that this stranger who rode for two hours with him in the backseat of a car didn't say one word until he did and then offered condolences about his father. What was that about? Paul pulled two one-hundred dollar bills from his wallet, handed them to the driver, and got back in the car. Patient, but still wired about this old man, Paul was able to let the driver finish hotboxing his cigarette. If he wasn't rattled about what just happened, he'd tell the guy he could smoke in the car if he wanted. Paul didn't mind. After all, he needed information from him.

When the driver was in and they were back on Route 64, Paul leaned up a little from the backseat, eyed the fixed on placard above the glow of the radio numbers. Ron Everson.

"Hey, Ron."

Ron turned his head as if to say, how in the hell do you know my name? Paul pointed at the placard and Ron nodded. "Oh yeah," he said.

"Who was that old man who rode up with us? Did you notice how he didn't say a word all the way up here and then got chatty once we made it?"

"Well, all I know is Caleb back at the office said he was a Harper guy. Papers are back at work. Like I'd tell you his address and everything anyway, buddy. That seems like something I shouldn't do. How about you just sit back and relax. I'll push it to sixty-five instead of the fifty-five the company makes us cruise."

So Paul tried to relax. He thought of what he'd ask Hill, who would absolutely make fun of him for turning around and coming back from Lexington. But this old guy Harper said it clearly.

Ask your Uncle Hill.

"Can you tell me where you picked the guy up at?" Paul asked.

"Buddy, I already told you. No address. Relax."

So Paul kept trying to relax. That's all he did as they drove the Mountain Parkway and then past Salyersville. He still wasn't relaxed when he was dropped off in Red Knife. He would go up to his grandparents' house and put away his stuff. Take a melatonin tablet and sleep a couple hours. Then he would find Hill. Get this bug out of his ear.

4

Paul's family was the kind of people that when a member who had been gone for very long returned, there was a large fuss made of it. Even if they came after a long while and then left and returned again shortly after, another fuss was made because they had returned after leaving again. The short of it was that the act of arriving, no matter how long a member had been away, was something to be celebrated. Other families, Paul noticed, did not necessarily do the same. So when he came back through the door of his grandparents' house, and especially since many of his family were still there talking after the burial, there was a second celebration for his second arrival.

His aunt said over and over she was glad he had to come back, that it didn't matter what for, because she hadn't had the chance to talk with him at the funeral. His cousin from Michigan, Jack, was ecstatic because there was a song he had wanted Paul to teach him, a song David used to play called "Memphis" and for sure the opening riff.

And on and on it went like this and all the while Paul stood around or sat at the end of the kitchen table or played the obligatory song on the Gibson flat top of his grandmother's. The sad thing about how his family was the type to welcome back with nothing short of a return party was that it was something they did because they weren't really all that close normally. It was a tradition developed from guilt. It was false, but still felt nice.

Now Paul really only wanted to get some rest and then look up Hill the next morning. By eleven that evening, family had thinned out. Only his grandparents were left, sitting at the kitchen table having another cup of coffee. The quiet was terrible after the activity for the past several hours. Paul heard every creak of the house settling. His grandfather scooted his feet across the floor and it sounded like someone moving furniture.

"Eve, I think it's about time for bed," his grandfather said. "This old boy is tired and hurting in his heart. But right now, more tired." Then William Shannon looked at him with a firm gaze. "Pray for us, Paul. Pray that we can sleep. The last two nights we've only had a couple hours sleep and it was all nightmares. Dreams about your dad, when he was healthy and young. You should have seen him then. But then me and your grandmother would wake up and he was gone all over again. It was a waking nightmare, Paul. Pray we can sleep."

His grandmother's eyes were more than weak. They seemed to barely stay fixed inside the sockets, so watery they seemed fluid and ready to simply pour out onto her cheek as a single large teardrop. "Pray for us all, Paul. You get some sleep, too. You need to rest, baby."

His grandparents met as William Shannon and Eve Sherman when they were both eighteen. All these years later Blue Boy and Pink Girl were still beside one another and tonight was no different. They stood together and walked from the kitchen arm in arm. For the first time since he came in for the funeral, Paul felt tears building up under his eyelids. When they were gone, Paul found a box of Benadryl and took ten of them dry.

Paul was asleep inside the stale covers of his father's bed when someone knocked at the front door. He slammed the palm of his hand on the nightstand and disappeared under the covers again. The knocking started again. He pushed the covers off his head and waited to see if his grandmother or grandfather would answer. When they didn't, he tossed his legs over the edge of the bed and started through the house.

His grandparents' bedroom door stood open four or five inches. Through the opening he saw them in bed, his grandfather rolled to his left and his grandmother flat on her back. Above them were the portraits of Blue Boy and Pink Girl. Paul wasn't sure these were the names of the two pictures. They had always hanged there, Blue Boy above Papaw's head and Pink Girl above Mother's. Both twitched in sleep and seeing them labor in that way issued a deep sadness inside Paul. Their baby boy was dead and, yet, they had to rest, had to keep moving on with their lives, eating, talking, breathing. He felt sadness and a burrowing guilt for having been so irritated for having to answer the door.

The knocking started up again. He continued down the hallway and turned the corner into the kitchen. He looked ahead through three slices of window in the top half of the door and saw three jagged parts of someone. The person was so tall he could not see the color of their hair. All he could make out was a nose, a mouth and a chin. He could see the man was rocking back and forth in front of the door.

"Just a minute!" he yelled across the kitchen.

Paul pulled the door open and saw the full figure of a man who easily stood six and a half feet tall. The man's face was docile, soft blue eyes and thin lips. He had a crew cut and twin receding hairlines arching far back away from his forehead. What was left was a patch of sandy blonde hair in the middle. When the man saw Paul, he smiled. His small mouth stretched into a big toothy grin.

"Is David home?" he asked when Paul had the door open.

He had the voice of a singer, a bass or a baritone, and right away Paul didn't know how to answer.

"I guess you should step in for a minute," Paul said. "Were you friends with my dad?" Paul couldn't think of anything else to say.

"I sure was!" The man said. He clapped his two huge hands and rubbed them together.

Paul stood in the doorway, waiting for him to come through, but the man stood in place, rocking back and forth on his feet and rubbing his hands together. Paul extended his arm like a butler would in an old movie, but the man still didn't move.

"I was your daddy's best friend! My name is Larry Fenner!" He offered the huge smile again. Most of his front teeth were rotten and one of his eyes flashed around in the socket, jerking back and forth in a nervous blur.

Paul pushed his back against the door, the hinges popping as he did, and Larry Fenner eased his bulk into the kitchen.

"Larry Fenner!" Larry Fenner said again. Once inside, he sat down at the kitchen table. His knees popped up to the edge of the table. "You mean your daddy never did say nothing about Larry Fenner?" He seemed shocked, maybe a little hurt.

Paul figured he had avoided telling him about his father long enough.

"Larry, my father passed away. Just this past week," he said, and then added, "I'm sorry."

Larry dropped his head and seemed to concentrate on his meaty hands, which he had been wringing together without mercy since stepping through the front door. He grinned again, this time not as largely, and the skin around his eyes seemed to weigh more, gravity pulling his enthusiasm downward even while he pushed through a smile.

"Your dad, Dave, would put your butt in the

sling if he heard you saying it like that. Passed away."
He stared off into the distance and lowered his voice to
a whisper. "People don't pass away. They're not like a
bad smell or campfire smoke. People die and that's the
way it is."

Paul felt his lips hanging from his face, his
mouth hanging open more than he would have
admitted. Somehow he was distracted for the moment
from his single-minded need to talk to his uncle. The
first time since the old man had spoke his last words in
Lexington.

"That's what your dad, Dave, used to say," Larry
continued, and then placed his red-raw hands in his
lap and went quiet. His eyes moved constantly. They
seemed to follow patterns floating somewhere in his
field of vision before settling on Paul. Paul could see
pain there, barely floating in uneasy blue waters. "I was
his *best* friend."

5

The day the boys decided to skip school was the hottest of August on record for Red Knife. It was a record day that stood until a full three decades later when in 1997, it broke 105 degrees in the second week. On this day, temperatures soared to just over 100 degrees several times, even during the morning. It was too hot for school, Dave Shannon told his brother, Hill, and their friend Tommy Spencer. He had a better idea, but it was agreed they should have a fourth man.

Truth be known, every one of them would have preferred to stop by Angel Burchett's house and ask her to go with them out to the old tipple, but Larry was the more realistic choice. Angel was in school anyways, the good girl. All three had been fighting for her attention for the past two years. Sometimes they passed the hours during summer break recalling which features they most adored in her. David never failed to mention her chestnut brown eyes, like pieces of toffee, he would say. The others fawned over the shine her dark hair had when she stepped from the Red Knife Public Pool. They kept the really gritty things to themselves, saving it for their private time. Tommy loved her laugh. He was always the first to mention her laugh. It soared from her and caught others laughing as it went. She was, they agreed, the only truly beautiful thing any of them knew.

But Larry was the choice. They all knew what he would be doing. It was Tuesday and Joe Fenner would have him out plowing the dry patch of land just in front of the clapboard house on Jensen Road. Tuesday was the day for turning the ground. It was never clear to any of the boys, or to Larry and maybe even Joe himself, if turning the ground during the summer and early fall months would do the garden any good, but it was either have Larry keep busy turning or have him laying around, into trouble.

Both Shannon boys were quiet. Tommy was quiet, too. All three had caught a good ride from Red Knife out to Jensen Road. It was a one-way trip, some guy heading to town with a load of fresh hay. Now the three delinquents leaned against the bare-branch fence lining Fenner's pitiful garden and watched Larry endure his father.

Sun glinted through a set of pine trees just above the Fenner's house and down onto a thirteen-year old giant dragging tired and enormous legs and feet through clump after clump of dust and brittle soil. The Fenner's horse rested under a makeshift roof connected to the side of the house. The horse's sides rushed in and out past its ribs and Dave noticed thick ropes of white mucus hanging from its flared nostrils. It could barely hold its head up and so the ropes of snot wobbled and spun in circles not more than an inch from the hard packed earth beneath the shed covering.

Larry could only have been so lucky. Maybe if he had started before the horse it would have been him the three boys would have seen under the shed trying to soak in the shade the way dry, summer riverbanks might somehow stretch toward a strong middle current. But Joe made him take second shift on the plowing, and it was this sad show the boys now sat watching, none of the three breathing very loudly, as if ashamed of the comfort they experienced while Larry tugged away at the plow straps.

The straps — thick, black leather, studded with brass fixings which seemed to boil into liquid beneath the sun — dug into Larry's back making red and irritated grooves well past the lower portions of his dinner-plate shoulder blades.

Larry tugged and breathed through his nose in massive gusts, blowing snot mixed with sweat across the dry earth. He didn't notice the three of them until he was near the west corner of the field. Joe had disappeared to the shadows of the front porch, lost in the cool shade, clutching a cold glass of water and rocking patiently in a wicker chair.

When Larry saw them, he forced a smile and then glanced back over his shoulder two, three times and hitched the straps into better position across his shoulders. David waved him over. Joe was already falling into an easy sleep in his chair.

"Your old man's about to nod off," Dave called to him. "Set them things down and get over here. It's an emergency."

Larry glanced again over his shoulder and then carefully, the way one might walk through a house at two in the morning after getting the baby to sleep, he stepped away from the straps. The plow broke through the dry field as he unhitched, spraying fine dust into the air on its way up and landed with a thud before coming to rest.

"We're taking off," Dave said when Larry made it over to the fence and rested his arms across. "Let's go. You have to go. I mean we skipped out on the whole damn day."

Larry shook his head and dug at his crewcut. There was dust and clumps of dirt sticking to his scalp which fell from his lowered head and drifted past the fence railings.

"You guys better just go on ahead and I'll catch up. Daddy's not bound to let me go much of anywhere today, you know, turning the field and all." He pointed with his head toward the mangled expanse of dirt behind him.

"He's asleep, man," Dave said, leaning in close to Larry. "Look at him over there."

Joe Fenner was now fully slumped in the wicker chair at the far end of the porch. Larry's mother was somewhere inside, busy at her own chores, pulling and plucking some type of vegetables and letting fresh meat of some kind simmer in a large black pot until it was tender enough to tear into pieces. Across his lap, the old man had a bamboo cane he had been given by Doc Bill Calup about ten years earlier to use after his tractor accident, except most everybody knew, especially Larry, that the cane was rarely used to help Joe along. Most of the time it was used in place of a whipping stick. Larry had the scars from blood whelps to prove it. They made crossed up lines past the small of his back, disappearing at his belt like white bumpy blocked off trails.

Hill knew that most of those whelps came while Larry plowed. He saw, on more than one occasion during spring planting time, Joe following Larry with the cane and pushing him and his plow forward, lash after lash.

"I know you're scared to go," Hill said. He had stepped in front of Dave and propped his arms up beside Larry's along the fence railing. "I don't blame you. Ain't none of us know what it's like. I mean we've been whipped some, but nothing like— " He stopped, aware that he had to be careful here. "Anyway, if you don't want to go then you don't have to. We're just saying it would be fun is all."

Dave perked up beside Hill.

"Yeah, Hoss, that's the thing. We just don't want you to miss out on the fun. Just like Hill said. See, we ain't told you where we're really heading have we?"

"I figure you're going down to Harper's to drink some," Larry said without expression. He didn't look up from his shoes.

"That's right," Dave said and smiled. "We're heading up to the Coal Tipple of Drink. Old Harper's."

Joe Fenner snored in from behind them.

A soft breeze cast its way through the small valley and dried the sweat across Larry's face. Hill stretched across the fence railing and patted the thick cotton sleeves of Larry's shirt and dust billowed away, caught by the breeze and carried away.

"Let's go, Larry," Hill said. "If he wakes up and sees you're gone, we'll take hell for it right along with you, all right?"

Larry studied this for a few seconds, working on the thought with great difficulty. "You guys won't get what I'm gonna get, but that's all right. You'll get what you're used to and that's bad enough, I guess." He stared again at his boots and swung one long leg over the fence railing.

The four of them left laughing and joking under their breath sliding down the grassy hillside leading to Larry's house. Joe Fenner was left to sleep and dream of ripe tomatoes, rows of corn, and farmer's daughters without last names.

It was a good walk to Harper's Tipple, a fixed monument to a once prosperous coal mining operation owned by businessman George Harper. During most of the 1950's, Harper and his three sons ran the most successful business in the eastern part of the state. The Harper family had tapped into a nice thick coal seam and made money hand over fist, but most people only knew this through curious gossip and mildly exaggerated folklore. The Harpers were humble people, the type of family who shined on Sunday morning in freshly pressed suits and new shoes, but who were always found through the week in work clothes and coated with dirt, grease or oil. Mother Harper was the most admired cook in her church group, often filling three tables at local funerals with dumplings, cakes and homemade mashed potatoes.

In short, the Harper family had been wealthy.

The Shannon brothers and Tommy used a latch safe at the top of the tipple as a place for storing beer and cheap liquor for the past year. The Harpers were long gone. George Harper suffered a stroke in the summer of 1968 while driving north to a meeting with investors. His oldest son, Matthew, had been with him when his truck veered across the center line and dropped into the river two miles from the market. Matthew Harper was twenty-six and had been married for eight days.

The rest of the family seemed lost after that. Two months later, Mother Harper passed on to follow her husband and oldest son, some said suffering from little more than a broken heart. The remaining family members moved north, but, to the luck of Hill, Dave and Tommy, did not sell their home or their land. Instead, the Harpers just moved away, lifted like a crying breeze away from what must have been the epicenter of their grief. The youngest son, John, loaded the last of the family belongings.

The dynasty was over.

It was George Harper's tipple, a 75-foot reminder of a humble, hard-working empire resting against the hillside ridge near the house, the boys first saw when they turned across the massive field to the south of Red Knife. Second was the mound of remainder coal left to gather decades of moss and grass at the foot of the tipple, and third, the hazy outline of the Harper house through the row of evergreens the family planted for privacy.

The house was modest and, compared to the tipple looming in the background, not what most would have expected. Larry swiveled his head and shielded the cresting sun with one hand. The other hand rested on his hip. He was still breathing hard, winded from his work, panting and frothing a little like the horse back home without the benefit of shade. He looked at the rattletrap metal step ladder connected to the side of the tipple and tried to forget about his father, who might have already woke up to discover him gone. His mother would likely catch a beating in his place, something Larry thought the others didn't know about. Just the same, he started toward the ladder without saying much. Dave and Hill fell in behind him and Tommy brought up the rear, never really comfortable, he said, with having anyone climbing behind him.

"Get your tremblin ass up here," Dave called back at Tommy. "Look at Larry."

Larry had already cleared half the tipple. His weight caused the ladder to sway back and forth some and the group could hear Tommy's breathing go from fast to slow each time Larry lurched forward for another rung.

It went this way, slow and steady, until the four reached the top. Hill was the second to settle himself along the top of the tipple. Larry had already disappeared around the wraparound runway circling the tipple's peak in the direction of the lock safe. He didn't drink, but he was always the first to get to the top and made his way quickly to the side of the tipple facing away from town. Across that horizon was a world of milk and honey, Larry would say.

"I got your milk and honey right here," Dave would usually say back, while turning up a pint of dark whiskey or a can of flat beer.

And it was the alcohol the rest of the group immediately went after. Dave in the lead, with Hill and Tommy behind him, made his way around the opposite side until all three came to a rest on their knees in front of the lock safe. It wasn't much really, just a portable locker turned sideways, what some would call a footlocker, maybe, but Dave had fitted the latch with a Master lock. It held with little problem two six packs of beer and three pints of whiskey, or a couple of fifths, if the boys could come up with the money and opportunity. The catch, of course, was that it was all hot. It was really hot during the summer and cans of beer would tend to burst from pressure if not taken out for a couple of days. But during the winter months, the beer would stay so cold that Tommy would joke it could make a man's teeth bust down the middle.

Tommy learned that phrase from his father,

Stanton. His father was a professional drunk, a man all the boys looked up to then and would later condemn as a street corner bum who would later be dubbed Piss Pot for his lack of bladder control in public places. However, this early introduction to how sweet an ice cold beer could be was marred during this time because along with the natural refrigeration came thin, crystal-specked ice which clung invisible to the metal rungs of the step ladder.

Standing on the tipple, the boys couldn't tell anything about the condition of the present stash — a fifth of Jack Daniels stolen from Tommy's father and four cans of beer saved from two weeks ago. This was because Dave, who had been digging through his pockets since dropping to his knees in front of the safe, could not come up with the key and had started swearing, at first in only half-muttered "shits," and then finally in stentorian bursts of purely imaginative foulness.

"Tell me you're just dealing with a bad case of crabs," Hill said and bent down to look close at Dave's twisted sunburned face.

"Crabs!" It was Larry from the other side where he had taken a long overdue seat. He pushed his tired legs over the edge of the walkway and seemed to be watching them dangle far above the ground below. Now he was craning his neck to see the others.

"Not those kind of crabs," Hill said and laughed. "Jesus," he said under his breath to Dave and Tommy.

By the time the three boys made it around to

where Larry was sitting with his legs hanging over the side, Larry had started to nod off to sleep.

"You're gonna fall one of these days doing that," Dave said, and then stopped at his side. He stared down at the pile of coal below them and studied the landscape carefully. "We need something to get this lock off," he said.

No one offered a suggestion. Tommy was thinking about how good even a hot beer would taste, while Hill sat down beside Larry and leaned against a portion of the railing. The metal walkway was still warm from the midday sun and he understood how Larry could have dozed off. Then, just as Hill was about to fall the opposite direction and land flush against Larry, Dave clapped two hands on his shoulders.

"I've got a plan," he said.

6

"Who's in there?"

A voice, soft and faint, came from the master bedroom of the house that William had converted from an embarrassingly small barn just after his retirement in 1976 from Inland Steel. He built the house with his own two hands, with a couple extra sets coming in the form of two strong and able sons willing to do anything to impress their father. David had once told Paul that his father, your grandfather, he would say, never loaded one shovel of coal. He would make it clear that William Shannon had been the best electricity man in three counties.

"They paid him over fifty an hour just to sit around in case something went down," David would tell Paul. "Fifty an hour to sit and drink coffee and watch other guys hump it out. And when something did go down, like part of a belt line or a burned up engine, Daddy would have it back up and going in an hour or so and be back in the break room sipping coffee and reading scripture."

But David always reminded Paul that his father, your grandfather, hadn't made it to that point without hard work. He'd tell stories about how his father had started with Papaw Payne in the mines when he was just eleven years old, a brief training period before he went full time at fifteen as the head underground electrician. The barn William Shannon had built into a home stood as testimony to that work ethic and pride in a job well done.

When his grandmother called from the master bedroom a second time, her voice had gone from a whisper to a louder more inquisitive tone. Worried maybe.

Larry shifted his seat at the kitchen table. His wandering eye moved at twice the speed of his good eye, glancing from Paul to the doorway leading to the hallway. He stopped rubbing his hands together and switched to sliding them up and down his shins and calves.

"It's Mamaw," Paul told Larry. "She's been sleeping, you know. She's real tired. I'll tell her you're here."

Larry straightened up in his chair. He pushed his barrel-sized chest out a bit more and absently ran his fingers and the palm of his hand across his burred head. He had been called more than a scoundrel more than once by Eve Shannon while growing up with David and the rest and didn't care to start again on his first visit in so many years. He hoped, without realizing the extent of what he was hoping for, to seem respectable to the woman who had fed him many nights after his father had ran him off for some forgotten wrongdoing.

It would be this memory of Larry's enormous appetite that Eve would remember when she turned the corner into the kitchen, tugging at the corners of her green satin house robe with one hand and tugging at strands of sleep-addled hair with the other. She drew her eyes together when she came through the doorway and then stopped just short of Larry, who had, by that time, decided to stand up and place his own hands behind his back. He was standing this way when Eve extended her arms and smiled with a strong set of natural teeth.

"Larry Fenner, Larry Fenner," she said. "Where have you been?" Her eyes were bright at the sight of one of her son's old friends, but beneath the warmth and kindness, Paul could see the tired look of a grieving mother. Paul wondered if Larry could see the same thing. "Would you like that I cook you something?"

At this point Paul realized that people will generally fall into an old pattern when faced with revisiting a person from the past. Long lost brothers, reunited on national television, will hug instantly, hug a stranger, whether from a sick need to please the corporate sponsors banking on a tear-jerker scene for the viewing public or from the innate urge to embrace their brother. Sometimes people just settle back into their positions, sometimes without ever haven taken those positions.

Paul thought about this while he watched his grandmother muscle her way to the stove, grabbing coal black skillets and silver pots which smelled of grease and some distant food, maybe bacon from that morning still lingering despite the clean washing given that afternoon. Larry seemed to either smell something or was simply remembering the numerous gangster meals Eve had fixed for him and the boys. David, Larry would explain later, had started calling them gangster meals.

"Mom will make us a pot of spaghetti the size of this room and enough homemade garlic bread to last a month, just like in the old gangster movies down at the Strand, just wait and watch," he would say during a long camping trip or an afternoon fishing. And it was always there. Today Larry was having thoughts about those meals, Paul figured, and then realized that his own stomach had started growling.

Without saying much, Eve had already moved closer to the stove. She turned the back left burner on medium heat and placed the five pound skillet squarely in the middle. "Let's make some hotcakes. I know it's not morning, but some of us have been sleeping the rough off this afternoon and probably need a little nourishment." She paused, hovering over the stove with a canister of flour gripped between her frail hands and lowered her head just slightly.

Larry got up slowly from the table and moved past Paul, who had positioned himself protectively behind his grandmother. She had fainted three times during the funeral, gripping doorways and begging her family to not make her leave her baby boy. But Paul was moved out of his place by Larry who nestled up behind Eve and wrapped his huge arms around her. Paul could see his grip startled his grandmother, but could also see that she welcomed the embrace.

"I'm sorry about my friend Dave and your boy Dave," he said. He waited and looked as if he might say more, but then moved back to the kitchen table.

"Ain't but one man suppose to wrap his arms around my wife, Larry Fenner, and that's me."

William stood tall in the doorway. He must have been a towering man in his prime, maybe taller than even Larry, but now he seemed weak. Maybe from the inside was where his weakness revealed itself, because on the outside he was hard and rugged. Paul walked across the kitchen and hugged him, amazed again, just like always, of how the muscles he felt under his hand felt like rock, or old leather.

"Hey, Paul. What'd you drag in with you here? Today's Tuesday. We're supposed to take garbage *out* on Tuesdays, not bring it *in*."

Embarrassed, but aware of this gray old man's sense of humor, Larry eased himself out of his chair again and stuck out his hand. William pushed a hand mangled with severe twists and smooth, shiny scars from years of generally harmless 110 volt electric shocks into Larry's and smiled softly. With this small movement, Paul could smell English Leather aftershave float through the room and then another smell that reminded him of his bus ride into Red Knife — the smell of hard work pressed into the fabric of clothes with sweat and salt and warm, summer sun. When his grandfather spoke again, he could hear a low rattle from somewhere.

"What've we got cooking here, guys?" William said. He also began moving across the room toward his wife. When he did, the illusion that William was still a hard man capable of sixteen hour work days was cracked, if not shattered. His steps were slow and deliberate, and then, as if this hint at a more realistic condition opened other windows, it became painfully clear to Paul that his grandfather had taken the death of his son in less stride than his strong will and general sense of pride had revealed. There were dark circles under his eyes and it seemed to Paul that he had lost thirty pounds in the last week. Paul wondered if he had even stepped into his father's old room since the horrible morning discovery.

"I am sorry about your boy," Larry said. His voice took on a lower tone, more baritone than before. "It hurts me, too, Mr. Shannon. I was Dave's best friend.'

William turned to Larry then, stared at him the way Paul thought he might have stared at a pesky radiator on the blink years before on the job. "Yes, David could have used more friends, but none as much as here lately. It seems the ones he did have just had other things to do for the past twenty years." He threw his arms up in the air, signifying all the other things there must have been to do. "Where exactly have you been all this time, Larry? Why haven't you came to see

David or Eve or me? Lord knows we kept you like our own child while your daddy…" He trailed off, catching his tongue with some effort. "Anyway, it's good to see you, now."

Paul wasn't surprised that his grandfather didn't mention his father's death.

"Let's eat," William said. "Can you still put down a stack of hotcakes a foot high?"

Larry nodded absently. He was picking at his elbow and his eyes were scanning the table cloth. He noticed the others watching him, Paul with his gaze trying to figure out a piece of family folklore now suddenly manifest, Eve cooking contently, lost in her work, and then William sitting across from him at the table with his hands crossed in a familiar praying position, and for all Larry knew he could be praying. He had seen Dave and Hill prayed over many evenings while staying overnight and letting things cool off at home. But now he was just worried if they noticed him counting the corners of the table, or the ragged corners of the sunflower pattern placemats at five different locations on the kitchen table.

He looked at each place mat. Five, he counted. One, two, three, four, five. I will not count the corners, he thought to himself, and was then hit by the fear that he had mumbled the words out loud. He glanced around the room while scratching the lengths of his calves and around his ankles. It seemed that no one had noticed. He looked again at the place mat, scratched the lengths of both his calves again, digging in good and hard with his fingernails. He glanced first at the top right corner and said in his mind: one. He stopped then and looked around at Eve. She smiled and he smiled back. William was talking about his hummingbird feeders. He looked again at the mat, this time at the bottom right corner: two. Inside his head, he called himself terrible names, most of which he pulled from memories of arguments between his mother and father.

Paul noticed Larry jerk a little in his seat. He looked at the big man's face and saw something there which seemed out of place for someone just invited to an impromptu grieving meal. It looked clearly like frustration. Larry's eyes narrowed and his mouth, tiny when concentrating, had peeled back into a single line across the bottom half of his face. And he seemed to be studying the top of the kitchen table with an odd intensity. But Paul didn't speak up until he saw Larry's lips become relaxed and begin to move, forming words, talking to himself, and apparently not all too happy.

The charade was broken by William, who had also noticed Larry. "What in the world are you doing?"

Larry stopped, his eyes still fixed on the third corner of the third place mat.

"Huh?" His voice came from far away and he kept his gaze fixed.

"I said are you all right?"

Paul broke in, saying that he was probably just hungry, a long drive, and then whispered that the news was probably just sinking in. But he knew, and William knew, that something else was wrong. Paul couldn't have known the extent of how different Larry seemed, but William could tell. He had known Larry Fenner, the man who had once pulled a mid-sized utility pole from the ground in front of the county courthouse because his buddies had put him to a dare. Larry Fenner, the man who had streaked the Strand singing, "Oh Susanna" and then the same guy who sang his way out of jail three hours later.

Eve, who had been concentrating on not burning the last three pancakes and mostly oblivious to the small drama which had unfolded behind her, turned just as William was about to go into his theory of Larry's new transformation. She held two dinner plates full of pancakes. She placed them on the table and then went to the sink and drew out four more plates. William and Paul were both reaching for a fresh stick of butter when Larry brought the house completely down.

"Do these have crabs on them?" Larry asked, scanning the cinnamon brown surface of his stack of pancakes. He took his fork and picked each one off the next, lifting first one then another.

"What?" Eve asked.

"Can I catch the crabs off these?" Larry asked again, still picking at them with his fork. "You know, jumping crabs."

7

Paul shivered under the covers. He was wet and the towels he had taken from the bathroom to spread across the mattress in the middle of the night were no longer dry and warm. The urine had soaked through now and both of the large beach towels were as wet and smelled just as strongly as the bed.

He was naked under the covers and his particulars were the coldest part. He had grabbed an old blanket from the closet when he found the two towels during the night and had been using it in place of the other, which, like the mattress, was soaked yellow. Now he pulled the guest blanket up around his chin and tried not to think about being cold there. He watched the window and waited to see daylight.

But before there was daylight, and while the sky outside the window was still mockingly dark, Paul heard someone in the kitchen moving dishes and opening cabinet doors. A wash of artificial light came from the kitchen doorway as someone opened the refrigerator door. He knew it must be his dad and immediately ran a possible way of telling him about what had happened through his mind, but shoved it aside. It was something his mom would have understood, she had been dealing with his bedwetting since he was four. That was nearly four years of sheet changes in the middle of the night at least three nights a week — a lot for a mother to have to deal with. But it was no day at the park for Paul either.

He thought about this while watching the artificial glow from the refrigerator crawl the walls of his bedroom and then disappear, only to reappear in two or three seconds. It was his dad, standing at the door opening and shutting it and trying to figure out why he couldn't go to sleep. He wasn't even sure if his dad knew about the bedwetting.

For what seemed like a long time, Paul watched for daylight through the window and listened to his dad in the kitchen until finally he began to make out a mountain top in the darkness. The sky was no longer black and riddled with stars, but was beginning to show gray-blue signs of morning. It would only be a short wait before he could get out of bed and then later on take a nap or something to catch up on his sleep.

It seemed that morning would take forever to break. The room stayed at that half glow for what seemed like hours, until Paul couldn't wait any longer. He pulled himself slowly upright and only then noticed that the wetness from the bed had crept up his back, nearly between his shoulders. If he were to take a shower this early, his dad would almost certainly hear and then be outside the bathroom door, banging away, but he could smell himself and the scent was making him sick.

He moved with the shadows through the

hallway leading to the bathroom door, wearing only his underwear and stained yellow and wet and cold, soaked and sticking to his skin. At last his hand was on the doorknob and then there was a sound from behind him so he turned the knob and pushed in one motion and nearly landed in his dad's lap.

There was David Shannon, bleak-eyed and unshaven, sitting on the toilet. In his lap was an open algebra textbook and on the floor beside him was a notebook covered in spiking hieroglyphics tossed onto the page in bold blue and black ink.

"I believe if I'd had a good teacher in high school I could have learned this," he said, still looking down at the book. No attempt to close the door back or a yell telling anybody he was in the can. "It's hard trying to teach yourself." He broke off as he raised his head and saw Paul was still standing in the door, unable to move away. He was glad that his father would finally know. "What the hell?"

At once he was self-conscious again, no more glad feelings. His dad was now standing and looking directly at his son's underwear. "Did you piss just now? Why'd you do that?"

Paul didn't' say anything. He pressed his thighs together and covered himself as best as he could.

"Well, don't just stand there. Close the door and I'll get out of here so you can clean yourself up. Jesus Christ."

Paul understood fast that he was going to be able to get around his problem of explaining to his father that he was a bedwetter. But then did he want to dance around it? It was eventually going to come to the surface. No need in taking more time with it than he needed to.

He closed the door and listened as his dad gathered papers up from the floor. Finally he heard the textbook smack together and then the door was opening. He stepped back and made up his mind.

"I peed in the bed, Daddy."

"What?"

"I peed in the bed. It happens sometimes." He was still holding to the front of his underwear and now his legs were shaking. They felt like slabs of cooler meat.

"You pee in the bed sometimes?"

It was strange to see an adult so confused. His dad stood with his free arm dangling at his side and the other clutching his books and papers. He looked like a freshman hunting for homeroom the first day of class.

Paul started to sidestep past him to search for a dry towel or sheet to stretch over the bed for the next couple of hours when he felt thick, square fingers bite into his upper arm.

"Not a problem," his dad said. "How long had your mom known about this? It doesn't matter, I know what to do."

He led Paul back through the hallway, past his grandparents' bedroom and into the kitchen. In the kitchen was a closet area that opened into a large space where the washer and dryer was kept. Above the washer and dryer there was a shelf full of cleaning utensils, powders and bleach. David grabbed a box of powders down from the shelf and plopped up on top of the dryer. He flung open the washer door and saw there was nothing inside. He turned to Paul, who was still standing behind him, now nearly crossing his legs.

"Go get your covers and sheets."

Paul didn't ask questions; he did as he was told.

"Now take those and put them in here," he pointed to the washer. "See that dial. You put that on warm wash. Come here." He grabbed Paul's arm and pulled it to him, winced at the smell that came from his body and put his hand on top of the washer. "Put them in. Now take that box of powders and pour out a full cup. Make sure it's a full cup. That smells like a latrine."

When everything was ready, he showed Paul how to turn the flat knob to the right to get things started. "From now on, when this happens, don't go get more clean sheets to put over it or towels either. Somebody has to wash that. Your grandmother ain't able to do that."

A week later at some dark hour of morning while Paul stood in the small space provided for standing in the washroom, he thought about how his grandmother couldn't manage to keep this cleaned up. And that's what kept him going. He didn't want to look at the clock. He was worried he only had a couple hours before daylight. He was sure clothes took forever to dry.

8

Going to Hill's was still the biggest priority, but it was nightfall now and Paul had, it seemed, a permanent traveling partner all of a sudden. Larry followed him across the street. Cramer's gas station was the only place to get a sandwich or something cold to drink after eight in the evening. To out-of-towners, Cramer's closed along with the other businesses in Red Knife at about eight in the evening, but Josh Cramer stayed around for awhile, talking and drinking, usually until about ten and then stumbled the mile and a half to his one-bedroom apartment in Beefhide.

His grandparents had gone to bed early. This left Paul to talk with Larry about any number of things other than his dead father. And now, long after their conversations had started, Larry busied himself with telling Paul stories about when they were all younger. When the two of them stopped just inside the gas station door Cramer peered out from behind his coal stove in the far corner. They had stopped after stepping in to shake off the fall air and now Cramer was squinting his eyes and looking closely at Larry.

"Dave just asked point blank if they had his mannequin," Larry said, still not taking notice of Cramer staring at him from the corner. "He said, 'I have a missing person complaint,' Just like that. A missing person." Larry smiled and then started laughing. He held his stomach. "Like it was real or something. And he was serious as a heart attack, too."

"Larry Fenner?"

The muscles in Larry's face jerked a little and his nervous eye jittered inside his skull at a faster pace than normal. Cramer was now sitting up straight in his oil-smeared chair. His body was bent. He was quite old and his sight was failing.

"Larry Fenner?" he said again.

"Hello, Mr. Cramer," Larry said.

"Jesus, boy. Where have you been?"

Larry's voice went down a notch or two, the baritone that had crept out while he was telling his mannequin story was now drawing back into his massive chest. He became a paradox, a large body, small approach. Almost apprehensive.

"I've been around," he said quietly. "I came in to see Dave, but, well."

"Yes, I know," Cramer said. he shuffled his feet across the gritty, concrete floor and turned to Paul. "Sorry as hell about your dad, son." He stopped and pulled at the brim of his cap a few times, three tugs and then a pause. "There is a little something I should bring up. I know it's not the right time and all, but you know how it is."

Paul was sure he didn't know how it was, or what it was for that matter. "What?" he asked. He tried not to sound defensive. Reacting to different comments since his father's death had become his forte, his own Shakespearean opus, and, although he was growing tired of the constant pressure connected with each encounter, he was beginning to learn how to spin each into whichever direction he found would provide him the quickest escape.

"David had a pretty good size charge account," Cramer continued. He allowed the words to settle in the air, dead and inappropriate. "It peaked at just over six-hundred last month and he paid it down some. I think to about four-fifty or somewhere around there."

Cramer walked with a noticeable limp since the back tire of a Ford Pinto had dropped across the bottom half of his leg during an oil change in 1972. He shuffled across to where Larry and Paul stood at the front door. Larry moved with him, passing him and continuing to the snack counter where he pretended to struggle with whether to take a fudge round or a raisin cake. This left Paul and Cramer alone at the front.

Paul had just received a raise three months before, but had taken the bonus that accompanied the pay increase and deposited it in a savings account. As Cramer stood in front of him, leaning on his good leg, Paul remembered the money Hill gave him at the funeral. It was still inside the Mason jar in his father's old room. If he remembered correctly, it had been about two-hundred dollars.

"I have some I can put on it now, but I'll need some time on the rest," he said.

Cramer nodded. Good enough for now, the nod

said.

"Here, that'll about do it, won't it?" Larry said. He had come up behind Paul and poked his hand around in front of his chest. Paul looked down and saw five one-hundred dollar bills sitting neatly in the palm of Larry's outstretched hand. "That'll make it even won't it?"

Paul was stunned. Before he could manage to decline the offer, Cramer swept the bills into his hand. "Yeah, that covers it. Now, what can I do for you boys?" He smiled at them then touched his bearded chin and looked again to Larry. "I remember that time up there at Harper's Tipple, you know that, Larry. You remember that summer?"

Paul, who was still thinking of how to thank Larry for paying his father's old gas station tab, caught the name Cramer had mentioned and forgot, for the moment, about how to settle up.

"Harper?" he asked, feeling the name with his ear, trying to figure why it was familiar. "What's Harper's Tipple?"

"Now that's a story Larry here might not be so happy about relating," Cramer said. "But I guess you ain't the one exactly asking about the story are you?" He glanced at Larry who had turned away from them and was counting square designs across the front desk that years of waiting customers had scrawled out in blue and black ink while their oil was being changed. He had his head ducked far below the rise of his chest the way a pigeon might or a duck or maybe an ostrich.

"Harper's Tipple is just up the road a piece here. I can't believe that all the years you spent here with your dad that you never went up there. It's just about two miles past the mile marker." Cramer paused and wandered back to his place beside the coal stove. "Your dad and uncle and that boy who used to live up around the Pines. What was his name?"

"Tom Spencer," Larry said, even more quietly than before, nearly whispering.

"Yeah, Tommy Spencer, Stanton Spencer's boy. Your dad, your uncle Hill and that Spencer boy would take bootleg liquor up there and get stone drunk." He stopped and laughed, clearly pleased with this memory, which had probably been buried for many years amid mental notes for various car repairs, payment priorities and customer phone numbers. "Sometimes they'd even take old Larry here. Anyway, the tipple is just part of the old Harper mine, but I guess it's about the most recognizable thing about it now that the house is about gone. The Harpers used to live there, surprise, surprise." Cramer stopped and laughed again at his joke. "Big family, lots of money, but good people anyway, you know."

"What were their names?"

"Who?"

"The Harpers."

Cramer rubbed his gritty chin again. "Oh, let's see, there was the old man, George, hell of a businessman, and then Mother Harper and I remember the oldest boy's name, the one that was killed with

George in the wreck, that was Matt Harper. And George had another son, the youngest, either John or Joe, I'm thinking."

"John Harper?" Paul asked.

"Yeah, coulda been it was John. He moved off after his daddy and brother died. I think the mama died just a little while after and then he moved. Came and got all the stuff out. Man, they left a good business! Wouldn't sell, neither. Believe me, I tried. So the whole thing went to shit after that. Nobody to run it, you know, keep it up." He stopped and pulled out a pouch of tobacco, pushed it with three fingers into the corner of his jaw, and spit flecks of black into the floor. "How come?"

"I met a man on my way back home from Dad's funeral," Paul said. "Do you think that could have been him, the guy you're talking about?"

Cramer scraped his boot against the concrete flooring of the front office and crossed his feet, one over the other. He looked at Larry, who was still eyeballing the countertop. Larry's fingers moved slowly over the counter and neither Paul nor Cramer could tell that he was counting dozens of scribbled squares and rectangles drawn by the hands of hundreds of people. Some were circles, drawn in pencil, and others were x's or just staggered lines, and Larry counted them all, grouped them into separate categories. He didn't look up at Cramer, but could tell from the corner of his jittering eye that he was watching, and, had he been alone with Paul, he might have explained what he was sure Cramer was about to say to him.

But Cramer didn't saying anything when he looked back to Paul. He only reset his gaze quickly back to another object, the checkerboard and then the row of Havoline 10W-40. These objects were less questioning.

Paul tossed his hand out from his sides and held them up in the air. "What? What is it?"

Now Larry stopped his counting, but he wasn't talking. He just glanced at Paul. He tried on a look that said maybe the best thing to do would be to drop it, but the look failed and it seemed to Paul that Larry was joining Cramer in the silent game.

"What?" It was less of a question now, more demanding, laced with far less patience. "What!"

"John Harper, the youngest son, didn't move off right away after all that sadness hit his folks," Cramer finally said. "It was a strange thing — I'm pretty sure he had that hearse sent out there to throw folks off. He was still there, and there for a good long while. Later on he moved out to Maysville. Only reason I know that is because Phillip Sherington was working in the deeds room for the county around that time. He told one person, they told two, they told six others. That kind of thing. He sold the property and the house to the county for development, which never happened, you know." He paused, perhaps for dramatic effect or maybe because he was just trying to think of the right words. "But now listen here, John Harper died not more than two years ago, and that's a fact."

Paul didn't even give Cramer's words time to echo from the corners of the matching concrete walls before he was slinging the door open onto the night air. "Bullshit," he spat. "Bad joke. Poor taste."

Larry jumped and caught the glass door before it shut and followed Paul out to the pumps and then across the parking lot toward the corner. The cowbell that hung from the station's front door shook violently just before the two cleared the corner of the building.

Cramer stuck his head out the door. "Dammit, Paul, go up there and get some rest. You got too much on your mind is all it is. Shit, I never said you was crazy! I was just telling the facts, that's all."

But Paul was already turning the corner with Larry close behind.

9

There was a small window in the kitchen situated just above where his mother once kept her spices and just to the left of a plaque fixed with a phrase he remembered from childhood. *May you be in Heaven a half hour before the Devil even knows you're dead*, the plaque read. John Harper smiled, brushed the plaque with the edge of one long fingernail, and leaned closer to the window.

The boys were back. The Shannon boys, Tommy Stanton and Larry Fenner, Joe Fenner's boy. They had started coming about two weeks ago, as soon as summer weather started in. He rubbed his chin and scratched his head and then started to the kitchen door that led outside. He stopped two feet from the doorknob, his legs numb, and then finally leaned against the wall. He braced his spindly frame with one arm and returned to the window.

The boys had come across the field in a mad rush, full of youthful impatience, and were now climbing the ladder to the top of the tipple. He thought again to step outside and call to them but this time only made it three small steps before moving back to the window. The curtains were pinned back from the window to let in some sunlight, but that was too high risk now. He pulled them slowly closed until he felt safely tucked away. Taking a glass from the dish drainer, he filled it half full from the tap and took a long drink. Water could sometimes help with the anxiety, stave off a panic attack. Another drink and another peek out to the tipple.

The boys had cleared the ladder. Now they bounced around on top of the tipple. Larry had wandered to the edge straight from the top of the ladder and was sitting with his feet dropped over the side. It seemed he was looking directly into the window. John backed up into the middle of the kitchen, losing sight of the boys for a moment while he considered the phone on the wall next to the refrigerator. It hadn't offered a ring in ten years, not once. He only used it once a week to phone in groceries and other supplies. He could call the sheriff's department and give a report. He wouldn't, he knew that, but he could if he wanted.

John knew the sheriff, a hateful but loyal man named Bob Tack Thompson. John's father had employed Bob's grandfather as a driver for two years. That connection alone would give him the open door to call and explain that some boys were out on his property, trespassing, he might say, and ask him to send somebody to take care of the problem. But that would involve a report, a conversation, maybe even a trip onto the porch, out of the sweltering furnace that was his house in early summer. It was complicated enough already, having to send payments for bills to keep up the house through Bob on the solemn oath and all his father had done for him that he would say nothing about his still living at the homeplace.

He returned to the window and took another drink of water.

The last time he was outside the house was at his brother's funeral. On the way to the church, his truck had stalled in a curve along Clark Mountain. The moments of the actual stall out was mostly a fog of panic and fear, distorted in his mind by his brother's death two days before and therefore distorted to him even now in memory. What happened shortly afterwards was clear in his mind. He could recall the headlights and then the sudden punch to his chest from the steering wheel, air escaping his lungs in a long whistle.

He opened the refrigerator. A pack of bacon and two gallons of milk sat alone on the top rack, one gallon that was two days old and the other apparently outdated that morning. He grabbed the most recent and took a glass from a nearby shelf. Inside were two bowls capped with hand towels and a block of cheese that had hardened to a rubbery cube; various, hard to discern items were shipwrecked along the bottom rack with a head of lettuce. Otherwise it was empty, filled more with blinking white light than anything else.

Returning to the sink, he propped onto his elbows and turned his attention back to the tipple. All the boys, save Larry, had huddled near the center of the tipple top. They were focused and seemed to be laboring at some task. Larry still sat plopped along the side with his legs dangling over. That boy's for sure going to fall, John thought, and reached in for the block of hard cheese. He took a knife from the drainer and pushed it through the tough center. He trimmed the hardened orange rubber away and made a second slice. What he was left with a half-inch thick section of the middle about the size of a money clip. He popped the piece of cheese into the side of his mouth. What he saw when he turned back to the window forced him to swallow prematurely. The Fenner boy was standing at the edge of the tipple. He had his arms held stiff to his sides.

10

Paul watched Larry's chest move up and down under the covers. He still hadn't went to see Hill. Larry had been his excuse for not going up to this point, but all along, if he was being honest with himself, a part of him didn't want to hear what his uncle had to say. So for now he watched Larry sleeping easily in the small bed beside his, the bed that used to belong to him when he was much younger. His dad's old friend breathed quietly, a slow rhythm, easy and comfortable.

Had Larry's life always been that way beneath the surface? In spite of all he had been through and been made to endure, had his inner mind, childlike and protected, managed to hang onto a peace not offered to those damned to ponder away those hours reserved for sleep? Larry continued with his peaceful rhythm and Paul tried to use its hypnotic quality to lull him to sleep. Larry Fenner was blissfully ignorant. This notion was only supported by the stories he had told Paul in recent days.

Most of the stories were not original to Paul. He had heard versions of them before, mostly from Hill, though his grandparents had told a few. But, despite the clear memories of those accounts, Larry's stories were different by degrees, such as his being asked to ride a twenty-inch bicycle across the rail of the train tunnel bridge. The story was familiar, but Hill's version had Larry volunteering to make the ride, in fact boasting that he could do it in record time. Hill's stories, he was beginning to realize, were full of embellishments, as well as the single detail of Larry choosing to do whatever particular feat in question. It was this common infraction that most often came out in Larry's stories about his times growing up with Dave and Hill Shannon. Much like Tommy Spencer, Larry fancied himself an honorary Shannon brother. But Paul had already allowed himself to, perhaps reluctantly, accept the fact that Larry was most likely less of a brother and more akin to a form of entertainment. A television show on tap, and live. Larry was probably a human distraction for the kids back then from what may have otherwise been a boring small-town life.

Paul, desperate for sleep but unable to bring together the positions needed for rest, or maybe simply unable to summon the peace of mind to close his eyes for very long, moved from his bed and nestled into his grandmother's rocking chair near the door to the bedroom. From here, rocking slowly, he drifted into a light half-sleep. He thought about the importance of small details, tiny infractions, and how they had started to accumulate clearly in what was the family mythology of Larry Fenner.

The next morning, lacking sleep but armed with

maybe the first clear and purposeful trip he had taken since arriving back in Red Knife, Paul left his grandparents' house early.

Larry was still asleep when he slipped through the screen door, holding it gently while it hissed closed. When he turned, he found had not gotten up early enough to avoid a bleary-eyed meeting with his grandfather.

William was in the front yard, bent closely to the fence, struggling intently with a row of waning fall beans. The vines had grown weakly, but persistently, through the mesh aluminum fencing and although fighting for survival, seemed to be losing. The leaves and vein-like vines were brown around the edges and generally gnarled together making any work to be done a losing fight.

"Where you headed to so early?" It was a strict question, less probing and more idle, but still curious enough to elicit a raised head and a halt to any more work to be done, pending an answer.

Paul stumbled rhetorically through a reply of some kind and instantly shifted his eyes toward the early morning sky, pretending to examine something there with great interest. But his light sense of guilt wasn't enough to keep from stepping around his grandfather and parting through the gate and onto the street.

"Paul. Now listen here." The voice again, this time from behind him, was forceful but technically void of overt authority, a gray area of emotion mastered from years of preaching in local churches in a town where men, sinning men, required prodding with a firm but gentle hand. "I'm going to tell Larry he needs to find him another place to stay for however much longer he plans to stay in Red Knife for all this business. He can maybe get a room at Conley's Motel or something. Point is, it's just time he moved on. Now you know what I'm talking about."

William was giving his grandson what mountain people called fair warning and felt that should be enough. It wasn't the first time he had been forced to move someone along before they were ready, someone who was brought in as a guest but then became a lingering presence. He had been forced to put many young men out on their ear when Dave and Hill were still at home.

And now, standing against the fence with a hint of what would quickly become afternoon sun pushing through the early morning fog and nursing an inherited case of messed and tangled hair, it seemed the same thing was happening again. Paul could have easily been his dad leaning lazily against the fence listening to instructions about putting out another friend who had worn out his Christian welcome.

William squatted against the fence, still holding three or four crumpled bean vines between his fingers, and took the opportunity to catch his breath. The fall breeze spun through the valley and relaxed him.

"I can take him today and help him look for another place to stay."

"Huh?" William gazed through Paul very briefly and then met him with a distracted glance. "Oh, yeah. Okay. All right."

Paul closed the gate to the fence and walked to his grandfather's car. He knew how to fix Larry's worn out welcome. He got in the car and headed in that direction now, sure that Larry would be sitting at his grandmother's kitchen table when he got back, waiting for breakfast but afraid to ask for it, trying his grandfather's patience, and still trying to understand where Dave was hiding.

11

It was nearly bedtime for Paul, but he wasn't sleepy. His dad paced through the kitchen, nervous and upset. His grandfather had just came in from his basement workshop. He wore a Core Company hat and a work shirt with a patch sewn above the left breast pocket. The patch said, *William,* and beneath that, *Head Electrician*.

He didn't say anything to Paul or his father when he stepped through the door. It was the first day of work for Paul's dad at a factory ten miles outside of Red Knife. He had already told Paul that he wouldn't be working the factory. He would be working security, making sure that while the workers were gone that nobody stole cable or other parts. He was going to be the night watchman.

Paul liked the sound of that.

It was five minutes before he needed to go and Paul's grandfather was supposed to drive him the ten miles out to Maysville.

"We need to go, Daddy," Paul's father said under his breath. "I'm gonna be late if we don't leave here shortly."

The old man eased across the room like cold molasses and poured a cup of coffee. He then went to the refrigerator and added nearly half a cup of milk. Paul watched from the breakfast bar near the front door. He had slipped behind the bar where strange and dusty artifacts had been stored many years before and found a large roll of yellowed paper. He recognized the paper from *Little House on the Prairie*. It was the kind the bald storekeeper always used to wrap meats and candies. He had rolled off about two feet of the stiff wrapping paper and located a box of assorted crayons from his toy box. He remembered the feel of the room, a feeling of anticipation, the way a family might feel in the minutes before leaving for a vacation. Except, in the unknown contents of his stomach, there was a sinking feeling. It was like a dream where you wake up one morning to find that the vacation left without you, somehow forgot you in the rush. He thought about this and drew a large, jagged circle with a red crayon, lightly, because he didn't have a peach crayon. He added two large ears and then made two smaller circles inside for the eyes. He drew a drooping arch of a mouth and then searched for a blue crayon while his father continued to pace behind him.

His grandfather had taken his coffee into the bedroom where he must have been changing clothes. He would drive his son to his first night of taxable work in five years.

Paul found the blue crayon and finished the picture with the addition of two sagging ovals dripping from two blue eyes. He worked quickly to color in the blue outline tears before his father came up behind him.

He put the crayon down and held the sheet of wrapping paper up, not saying anything, but letting the picture say its thousand words. His father only shook his head. His hair was stuck to his head and looked plastic, wet from a fresh bath, although it was an hour past Paul's bedtime. Thick strands of black hair fell loose as he shook his head, explaining to Paul without words that he had to go, had to work. It was a brief and wordless communication, but Paul started to cry, unable to hold back and preserve the silent understanding.

He watched the door close lightly behind his father and listened to the car pull from the gravel driveway.

Nine hours later Paul's father sat on the edge of his only son's bed. He watched the small smooth face lying still against the pillow, smiled when the tiny lips puckered in sleep, smacked together, and then became slack again. He rubbed his fingers through the fine blond hair and then leaned in close and kissed his forehead. He could smell shampoo and soap.

Outside, the world was waking up. Truck engines turned over stubborn and cold and started. Men who had been pulled from their beds for work coughed into the cold winter air, gripping cups of coffee like life lines, moving through the thick and dark morning like tired fireflies of struggling heat and discomfort.

His father's lunch bucket sat beside him in the floor, half empty. Dust was smeared across his face. Smears of it blotched his hands and covered his fingers. The ring Paul's mother had pushed onto his hand one day in July shot occasional glints of pure yellow across the room. His clothes smelled of rust and grease. In the inside pocket of his work coat was a piece of yellow chalk used for marking pieces of machinery that had cleared status checks during his shift.

"Hey little man wake up."

Paul moved sideways in the bed, yawned once. "Daddy?"

His voice was broken with sleep and muffled. He was tired but happy to see his dad home again. The torn illusion of security had now been stitched back together. When he did finally open his eyes, he had to squint because the room wasn't as dark as it had been just a couple of minutes earlier. Lights from a truck garage across the street had been turned on for the morning shift and the light broke through the window shades in split shafts of manufactured brilliance. When he saw his father sitting beside him, a tired look plastered on his face, he smiled and reached out to touch his hand. His father pulled his hand close into his and held it there softly. The comforting touch forced Paul's eyes closed again and before a few seconds had passed he was back asleep.

"Hey little man let's go outside," his father was whispering in his ear. "I brought something back from work and now we can play. Now we have time."

The clock on the wall to the right of Paul's bed said it was about a quarter to five in the morning. Paul couldn't see this. All he knew was that he was glad to see his father, but was sleepy and it was still dark outside. Darkness meant sleep. He wanted to tell his father they could play in the morning, but he was afraid. He could hear him still talking in his ear. He could sense irritation there and so opened his eyes.

Paul's father saw the tired blue eyes open and took the small hand gripping his own and pulled his son from the bed. Paul staggered to his feet, weaving in the middle of the room and wiping his eyes with the backs of both hands. He was in his underwear and the room had grown cold through the late hours of the night compared to the warmth beneath his blanket. He wrapped his hands around his elbows and blinked several times to clear his vision. When he did, Paul saw his father's face, stern now and maybe upset.

"You sure were awfully sad to see me going a little while ago to be standing there now acting like you don't even care what I brought home."

The words bit into Paul like brittle winter ice and he was afraid he would cry again. He saw that his father held the picture he had drawn for him earlier in one hand. When he noticed that Paul had noticed it, he dropped it into his lap.

"Forget it. I'm going to bed."

He stood up from the corner of Paul's twin bed with a creak of springs and slats and started out of the room.

In a sleep-crazed frenzy Paul searched the floor for his pants, found them, and quickly pulled them up over his hips. He ran through the kitchen to catch up with his father who was turning the corner into the hallway with his shoulders and head slumped almost comically toward the floor.

"What did you bring, Daddy?" Paul said. "Let me see. We can play with it now. Okay?" His tiny voice spread across octaves and cracked, splintered in his throat, lost and useless. His legs trembled and his feet ached against the cold of the kitchen floor. His eyes were wide open now, but streaked with red and dull.

His father turned in the doorway. He stood still, his hands down to his sides, and his expression changed from angry to hurt, and then he smiled, just a little. Paul walked through the kitchen, still holding his elbows in his hands. The corners of his mouth trembled for a moment and then spread into a smile of his own. Paul hoped his father couldn't see through that smile, at the sleepiness and dread.

His father wrapped his arms around Paul and Paul could smell the grease and rust and the mild odor of sweat. He jumped slightly as his father jabbed his hand into his coat pocket and brought out the piece of yellow marker chalk.

"Remember what we used to do with sidewalk chalk, Pup?" His father said. "This is the same thing. I brought it from work. It's the same kind. Come on."

Paul wanted to ask him to wait, needed to tell him that he had to put on a shirt and jacket, but his father was already out the door and he didn't want to watch his face, now a bright beam of victory, change back into hard granite, volcanic rock and lava underneath. Instead, he followed his father's excited steps out the door and recoiled from the wind and cold at once.

A thin frost coated the front porch and the tops of parked cars glistened and sparkled under the street lights. The only car on the street that wasn't covered in winter diamonds was his grandfather's, which had just dropped off his father moments ago. It was warm and ready to travel. Paul could still hear the motor ticking beneath the hood as they passed two oil spots to find a clear area on the pavement for drawing.

The wind and cold had already numbed his bare feet to the joints of his toes and turned spots along his skinny chest and arms bright red and blue, and all the time his father was still marching around in the center of the street hunting for the exactly right spot to start.

"I should go in and get a…" he started, but was interrupted when his father let out a cry of discovery and dropped to his knees, clutching the piece of chalk between two gloved fingers. Working frantically, dirty black hair moving wildly across the concentrated wrinkles of his forehead, he wrote in bold letters, pressing down so hard Paul could see tiny fragments of yellow shards falling to the sides.

BY PAUL AND DADDY.

His father stood up and handed the piece of chalk to Paul. Paul took the chalk in his hands and struggled to grip it between his fingers.

"Go ahead," his father said.

Paul crouched on the pavement and started a large circle in the middle of the road, arching his arm across half the street until he finished with a circle big enough for both he and his father to stand in. After a deep breath, he fixed his eyes again on the pavement and added two circles for eyes, a small and round nose, jagged and broken from what were now uncontrollable shivers running along his arms from his elbows to his wrists.

He then outlined a mouth, a sagging arch like in the wrapping paper picture earlier.

He didn't look back at his father, who was standing behind him breathing deeply. But if he had, he would have seen a familiar look spreading across his face, confusion, maybe, or anger. Instead Paul kept drawing. Two small yellow pupils and then two more symmetrical ovals under the eyes, dropped down onto the cheeks. It wasn't blue, but yellow tears would still explain what he couldn't say, just like before.

He stood up and felt his heart beating inside his heaving chest. He then turned around, the chalk falling from his grip, and then there was only darkness, spreading like ink.

12

Off Route 460 a dirt road led into a small valley.
Turning a natural corner of overgrown bushes, Paul
was stunned by the largest pile of abandoned cars and
trucks he had ever seen. He figured he hadn't seen very
many piles of cars and trucks in his life, but this one
had to be considered massive by any standard. To the
left of the pile, sticking up from among several heaps of
tossed aside engine parts, fenders, and bumpers, was a
splintered sign.

HILLMAN'S CAR & TRUCK PARTS.

The sign was made from scrapboard. The words
looked like they had been scrawled on by an eight year
old. It had been standing long enough to be tilting
noticeably to the left, surrounded by old grease,
buckets of oil, and assorted engine parts.

Paul pulled the car to a stop and got out. The
lazy sounds of a thousand insects from the twin fields
of wild grass lining the dirt road replaced the blare of a
radio advertisement. He stumbled across the road and
high stepped through the grass to the sign. It was
scrapwood, but had a familiar blue color Paul could
remember seeing when he was younger. He suspected
it could be one of Hill's old election signs that dotted
the county several years ago when he was still

practicing law. He cleared a mosquito infested set of tangled bushes and finally came to the sign. He avoided a puddle of thick grease and, leaning forward on the hood of a Ford Galaxy, craned his neck around to have a look at the back side of the sign.

It was an election sign. Across the top and in far better and much bolder white lettering were the words, *A Proven Choice for County Attorney,* and then below that, *SHANNON.* Paul gave the sign a couple taps with the back of his hand and started back to the car. Insects bit at his ankles as he went. As he crossed the front of his grandfather's car to get back in, he saw that about ten feet ahead the road sank and ran into a sizable creek. Beyond that, he could see the driveway leading up to Hill's place, a trailer that served as both home and main office for repair inquiries. In the driveway sat his S-10 pickup, which was covered from fender to fender in dried mud, likely from the creek passing. The water looked about three feet deep in places and Paul locked the doors, grabbed the keys, and split the weeds to hunt for a place to cross.

Hill stood in front of a grimy window in his trailer and watched his nephew prance through the weeds to a thin stretch of land peeking up from the small breaking waves. Paul lifted his legs gingerly and made his way across and Hill looked back to the car, shiny with wax. It was his dad's and Paul must have borrowed it for the twenty minute drive out here.

He ran his fingers through his hair hoping to force down at least two or three of the rat's nests that had formed during the night. He had heard the engine of the car going and thought it might be Dan Preston coming to pick up his alternator. All in all, he was happy to see Paul, but thought he had already went back to Philly. Hill found his work shirt from the day before and pulled it over his head, patted his hair down again, and started to tuck it in, but realized he was still wearing his jogging pants and thought better. When he stepped onto the porch there was Paul coming from beyond the grass. He threw up his hand and smiled. Paul was a good boy, always had been, somehow.

"Hey, long time no see," Hill called across to Paul when he was close enough. "You ain't been gone but a day or so. What's got you back here?"

"About the craziest thing you can imagine has me back here," Paul answered. Hill took Paul by the shoulder and they stepped inside the tiny trailer.

Hill's trailer always gave Paul pause when he first stepped in. Even as a kid, when he and the rest would come out to talk to Hill during the long nights when he would drink too much and talk even more. The defeated light yellow color of the aluminum siding and the rust framed windows with their bed sheet curtains was only a preview. Inside the trailer there would be more of the same. A scarred and chipped coffee table, maybe sitting upright or on its side, a host of leftover food adorning various kitchen utensils in a kitchen both too small and, for practical purposes, useless, since Hill never cooked but ordered food from a nearby pizza and sandwich place. And of course there were the books.

Paul knew the living room would be mostly books, save the coffee table. Indifferent about shelves, Hill had always stacked his books in the floor. You could quickly figure out where his favorite reading spots were by the number of books in a given stack. Beside the room's single chair, a ratty thing full of holes and covered in fabric course as horse hair, there would be a pile of books eight or nine high, required reading, he would say. Kierkegaard, Twain, Proust, and then a few of the contemporaries, and then back to the ancients, Plato, in particular, as a reminder of what true government could be with great vision.

"Hey man. I ever tell you you live in a grassy swamp?"

"You've mentioned it," he said and sat at the kitchen bar. "So you say your mom's hanging in there? I always liked Mary."

"Yeah she's up north. Moved about two years ago to be closer to me on the East Coast."

"See, that's what I'm talking about. Mary never did nothing that wasn't with you in mind."

Paul let that stay in the air a few seconds, looked around the trailer again, and waited for Hill to move along. If he thought too much about his mom, about all the days from the split until now, he might easily get emotional.

"What'd the letter say?"

"You know, the same stuff. You know how Dad

was."

"*Was*, yep. Man it's crazy to say *was*. I miss him a lot, Paul."

"You gotta be kidding, seriously kidding me. You don't have to say that on my account."

Instead of answering, Hill stood with his arms crossed and looked again out his dirty window. There was a spoiled food smell tearing at the small insides of the trailer like olfactory spikes of dull pain. In addition to the coffee table there was a desk in the middle of the floor. Thin squares of paper were scattered from corner to corner. A waste basket sat just off to the right of the desk and was adorned with a wrinkled bumper sticker.

Mays County has the best politicians money can buy, it read.

"Well, in the spirit of small talk, how's it going?" Paul said, leaning against the Formica island which served to officially separate the trailer's single room opening into a legitimate kitchen and living room.

"It's going." Hill rubbed stubble across his chin and made a few more attempts at getting his hair to flatten to his head. "You read the note I gave you at the funeral home, you say?"

Paul nodded. "Yeah."

"I didn't read it, by the way. I figured that was something between you and Dave. I don't know how much money was there and didn't count it, either."

"I appreciate you bringing it. I just wish you could've hung around a little while longer."

Hill plopped down in the chair, a comfortable

fit. "I would've, but you know how the fake can make a body ill. I figure I hurt just as bad here as there and here I've got my own peace of mind to comfort me. But then, I ramble. I figured you'd be gone by now."

"Yeah, I know." Paul moved his back muscles against the countertop and rubbed his own chin, less sandpaper, less life taken on the point of that chin. "Listen, I had something really strange happen when I got to Lexington. I'm just going to tell you, it's why I came back."

Hill had relaxed into his chair and cast his eyes out the window to the field beyond. Now he sat up and cocked his head to the side, looked across the room. "I'm all ears, as they say."

Paul went through the details of his trip to Lexington and the old man calling himself John Harper, that last cryptic suggestion. The way it came out of nowhere and how the man disappeared into the clinic.

"John Harper," Hill said. "You sure he said John Harper?"

"Yeah. John Harper. That's what he said. But this guy knows you, and he knew my dad had died. He knew *us.*"

"Well not the whole thing," Hill said. "Not really even close, truth be told." He let go a long sigh. It was the kind of sound a person made when giving up or giving in. One sigh was followed by another and he said, "Larry come in for the funeral?"

"He was late and I think he didn't know about

Dad dying. I think he was just visiting."

"I haven't talked to Larry since junior high school, the summer before we started high school."

"You've got a chance to catch up, if you'd like to."

Hill stared blankly across his living room. "What?"

"Well, he's been staying with me at Dad's for the past week. Papaw's getting that edge to him, you know what I'm talking about."

Hill nodded and then sat up in the chair and scratched the tops of his knees. "You've heard the stories about Larry, right? I know you have, because I've told a ton."

Paul stayed quiet. It seemed Hill was talking to himself more than anything.

"Yeah, Larry Fenner. He's been staying with me at Dad's, or Papaw's, but Papaw's getting a little fed up with him and I thought maybe he could, well, you know."

Hill just sat in the chair, not picking up on where Paul was going. Paul wondered if it was intentional or just more of the strange behavior he had taken on since Larry was first mentioned.

"Why don't you just ask him how much longer he's staying?' Hill said. He dropped back into the chair and looked out the window again, but his eyes didn't seem as far away this time. He was thinking. "This doesn't matter anyways. We might have other things more pressing."

"The deal with this old guy I talked to, for sure. But, to be clear, you don't want Larry to stay here?"

"I have to be honest, I don't know if I can. Me and Larry, well, I haven't seen him in a long time and even then we just weren't that close anymore."

Hill went to a yellow refrigerator that had, at one time, been covered in stickers, but was now bare, save some left over glue and white patches of stubborn paper. he opened the door and pulled out a liter bottle of orange juice. Paul could smell a dozen different types of food carry on the breeze from the door fanning open. Hill offered Paul a drink of orange juice he pulled from the insides of a refrigerator that looked worse than some cavities he had seen. Paul waved him off. Nothing that came out of that thing was going into his body.

"Did anybody ever tell you about Harper's Tipple?" Hill asked.

Paul shook his head.

"John Harper, the John Harper I knew, was George Harper's boy," Hill continued. "Incredibly wealthy man. He owned coal mines all over this region. Even had one on his own property after he found a good seam of coal there, which was some kind of mineral miracle, truth be told. Thus the tipple near the big house."

"They said his family used to own a business here a long time ago."

"Who said?"

"Cramer."

"*Cramer*," Hill said with thick contempt. "Maybe it's the same guy, but I heard he got killed," Hill said after a few seconds of silence. "Anyway, are you asking me if Larry can stay here?"

"Yeah, I guess so."

"Does Larry know about this? Larry might not want to stay here. Harper's Tipple might keep him from it."

"Well what in the hell happened at Harper's Tipple?" Paul couldn't hide the irritation in his voice. He didn't even try.

"What happened was I ran away, Paul. But then I'm good at that, or so people say."

"What's that mean? You run away?"

"You know what I mean. How I abandoned a good profession, lots of money and power, a good life."

Now it was Paul's turn to go quiet.

He knew most of his uncle's story. Hill had went to some religious-based law school in a neighboring state after getting an English degree that included a shiny collar at graduation for doing so with honors. He busted through his courses in short order, done the required reading and finished law school without so much as shifting his schedule once. He simply took what they gave him and came out clean, confident and ready.

Returning home to search for a place to set up an office was routine. He figured he would hang a shingle, make a little vacation money and then be out of the legal business and back in school. He wanted a doctorate in political science.

About two and a half years after Hill opened his office in Red Knife, Mays County Judge-Executive Crit Collins broke his hip outside a Dairy Cheer. It was November and Collins slipped on a patch of three-inch thick ice and pulverized both crests of his ilia. That's all people talked about for a month, and just like that. Women were stopping in grocery stores, *Did you hear about Crit? Doctors say he crushed both crests of his ilia.* Everybody felt like a doctor using the medical terms. Both crests of his ilia. It was educating, at least.

It was three weeks in the hospital and another two months of bed rest after that for Judge Crit. When he finally got up and about, a former lawyer himself, he went to Hill. The Diary Cheer was nailed to the wall and that was that.

Hill was a personal injury lawyer. A good one, and Crit knew it. He also knew Bill Singleton, the owner of the ill-fated establishment, was soft. The combination was lethal. Singleton hired a suit out of Crestville who buckled quick and before long, Hill was in politics.

At first he worked for about a week after winning the case for Judge Crit helping get the judge's paperwork back in order before he returned. In his absence, the county had lost three grants and blew a chance to annex a section of land valued for its business location potential. It took Hill about three weeks to get things straightened out and when the dust cleared, he had thrown in a renegotiation of terms that would ensure the county got the land. A telephone headquarters was built on the land about six months later, and when Jones Food Service moved out not long after, the phone company became the county's fourth largest business concern.

Hill was pushed into the top list of the county's political figures, without even holding an office. The following year, Hill announced his candidacy for Mays County Attorney and won during the fall race. It was and remains the largest voter turnout in the county's history, with more than eighty percent of the people voting, and most of them for Hill and whoever else Judge Crit backed.

Hill once said he slid into his spot on a firm handshake, a good smile and a concrete-thick patch of ice. But there was hard work involved, and, most of all, a hunger for the truth. Hill would never admit to the last, he would say it sounded too melodramatic, but most people knew it was true. Most people even understand what caused his breakdown and eventual resignation, as well. What people couldn't understand was the path he took afterwards.

His breakdown came, melodramatically enough, during a trial. Not a Perry Mason trial, those rarely happen in the real world, Hill often said. This happened during a trial where a couple was trying to get their insurance company to pony up money they promised on their policy in the event of an accident. Bill and Jill Morgan had been hit from behind. They had told the guy who hit them they were fine and the guy drove off. After he left, Bill called the state police and filed a complaint. It was a hit and run case. They caught the guy and got him on some kind of charges, and the Morgans contacted their insurance company.

No can do, they said. That's when Bill and Jill went to see Hill and, of course, Crit.

Bill had worked a card game with Crit in the seventies. One of the major players in that game was a doctor named Royce Pennington, who was what Crit liked to call dead money, an easy kill, just like the restaurant owner.

Crit convinced Royce to see Bill and Jill as patients, which basically consisted of the two of them sitting in his waiting room watching a talk show and reading copies of *Field & Stream* for about ten minutes and then talking to Royce for about two minutes, mostly about fishing and which school Jill got her accounting degree from. In and out, just like hundreds of others.

On the day of the trial Royce took the stand and testified that the couple had suffered severe injuries to both neck and lower back areas in such a way that it had affected their lives horribly, he said, just horribly.

Bill and Jill were going to be heading home with a little over two-hundred thousand dollars, after Hill's fee. Hill knew he had done absolutely nothing but known Crit and was going home with more than what most people were making for a year's salary in Mays County based on that affiliation.

People in Mays County knew it, too.

In a succession of split-second thought patterns, Hill decided he wasn't going to go through with the setup, hell or high water. While the jury deliberated, Hill crept away from his desk, past the judge and into the back hallway where the jury room was located. He stood outside the door for awhile, aware that what he was about to do would change everything, then figured it would change things for the better and opened the door. Twelve faces stared blankly up at him. Where was the bailiff? How did you get in here? You have to leave now. Leave now, Hill, and we won't say a word.

That was it. It was the final twist of his arm, and so he came out with it. You poor, poor people are dumb as a sack of rocks. He said it again and then a third time, tossing his hand through his forty dollar haircut and tugging away at his silk raspberry and black striped tie from Corner Street.

What followed has been retold through the circuit court circles time and again, avoided in conversation by most family members and changed Hill forever. The outcome of the case wasn't the point. Hill had changed the face of the game for himself. He could never be viewed as credible again. He had allowed a witness to take the stand and purger himself, knowing what was happening.

But he didn't mind. He wanted out. He wanted to do what he did best.

"Run away. That's what I did, Paul. From the courtroom then and before then on that day at

Harper's. It's the thing I'm best at, running away."

"Jesus, Uncle Hill. What about Harper's Tipple?"

"Well, you know, if you ain't got that story by now, I probably ought to leave it alone. That was something your dad should've told you about."

Someone knocked at the door and Hill shifted gears. He went from the serious tone he had kept with Paul back to the jovial junk dealer when he saw a familiar face staring through the screen door.

"Hey, James, it'll be a couple more hours. Just get yourself a seat there and I'll get back on it. Talking to my nephew here. You remember Paul."

Paul didn't know James and James obviously didn't know Paul or have any urge to correct that as he flopped down where Hill had just moved from.

"I'm gonna head on out," Paul said, and patted his uncle on the back.

Back up the dirt road he kicked loose gravel and picked weeds from the side of the road. He had to wonder what he was even doing here. He hadn't called work in two days and the last time he spoke with them, the best he could tell them was that it would be a little while longer. Somehow he doubted it would be enough to get them to forget about two days without a word. He had probably lost his job.

13

It was a Marlin .22 rifle. Simple, nothing special. Brown wood and black steel. Paul held it in his hands like a newborn and waited on the porch for his dad. Beside him was a box of shells. He plucked two out and rolled them across the palm of his hand.

His dad came through the front door and motioned for him and he followed. They piled into a dented pickup truck and rumbled toward Dealer's Field without talking. His dad looked sleepy, and kept reaching across the seat while driving and adjusting the gun so that the long black barrel pointed out the window instead of to the roof of the cab. Just before pulling into the field, his dad turned to him.

"Always point the end away from you or anything else. Point it in the air, away from other things. Guns can turn on you. Guns will bite you if you give them half a chance."

They left the truck on the edge of the field and made two sets of slick tracks through the frosted grass. His dad pulled a pair of thin leather gloves from his pocket and handed them to Paul.

"When I entered the military, they gave me an M16 assault rifle," he said. "They told me to keep it with me. I did. I kept it outside my shower and beside me when I went to sleep. I cleaned it every day, each evening. I learned that gun like the back of my hand. When I left the military, the last thing they took from me was that M16."

Paul looked across the field and spotted the wood rail they had put up yesterday evening. They had lost sunlight then, but today was different. It was warmer today, brighter. Rays of sun spiked through thin winter clouds, and Paul tracked across the field to place sixteen ounce pop bottles across the rail. He then paced the ten steps back to where his dad sat on the ground.

"We're gonna lose light if we don't get started," his dad said, and reached his hand out for the gun.

Paul handed it over and in fluid motions his dad popped the small black magazine clip into the palm of his hand and dropped it in his jacket pocket. He then pulled out another clip, a yellow clip that was much longer than the other.

"This is a banana clip. It holds more rounds," his dad said.

He handed the clip to Paul and watched him slide the copper shells in one at a time. Paul handled them like tiny sticks of dynamite, pressing down softly on each one until it clicked into place.

"I was what they call a high marksman in the military," his dad said and pulled the gun from Paul. He lifted it to his shoulder, aimed for the briefest second and then squeezed the trigger. Instantly one of the bottles exploded in a flash of sound. Shards of glass spun away. Layered clumps shifted and then dropped beneath the rail.

The cold and calculated accuracy of his father's shot stayed like a sunflash in Paul's mind. He closed his eyes and remembered the stance. Head tilted slightly forward, eyes lowered to the sites, left arm relaxed and bent, right hand -- the critical right hand -- tense and locked.

"Don't forget to keep your right hand gripped just a little. But remember, the trigger finger should be the most relaxed part of your body. You're gonna squeeze the trigger, not pull it. That's very critical. Okay?"

Paul nodded and took the gun back in his hands. It felt heavier now, and the smell of gunpowder was coming off it in waves. There were four bottles left.

"You'll just need four shots for this," his dad said. "Take each one out at the neck. That's what we'll call our head shot. Understand? Get that shot and you'll just need one bullet."

He raised the gun to his shoulder. At once his vision became blurry. In focus, out of focus. It felt like the gun had been pushed against his shoulder for an hour. The bottles looked like smudges across a dirty window.

"Jesus Christ, Paul." He snatched the gun out of his hands. It happened so fast Paul was left standing with his arms still in position, his legs still perfectly poised. He sucked in a fast breath and felt his heart start banging against the inside of his chest.

"Jesus! You'd done had your head took off. End of game! Understand!"

Paul muttered and nodded slowly.

"It's gotta be like this!"

Four shots rang out in quick order. The bottle necks split in half and toppled domino style onto the ground.

"What are you thinking about? They're just bottles. No pressure. And even when there's pressure, you've got to maintain. You can't lose it. Can't afford to." He grabbed Paul's arm. "Here, I'll show you pressure."

Paul was suddenly about to urinate and his bottom lip quivered. He hated that it quivered, and tried to stiffen it, only to make things worse. He felt his dad's powerful grip take hold of his arm and his body tingled at the touch. Marching him across the field, he positioned him in front of the rail. When he had him standing to his satisfaction, he turned and marched back the distance where they had been shooting. He paused, and took two more steps for added distance.

Paul could hear himself pleading, but the sound was low and pathetic and blended with other sounds, natural sounds coming from the nearby hillside and some place over the ridge where the lively hum of a car engine throttled up and down. Paul's voice was weaved into this, moving up and then down and then breaking.

"Grab the bottom half of the bottle in the middle, right there behind you, and put it on your left shoulder."

He grabbed the thick bottom half of the bottle, craned it above his head, and settled it into place on his shoulder. He then watched quietly while his dad gave the Marlin a shake, pulled the butt against his chest and steadied the barrel. At the moment Paul was able to steady his breathing a little, the bottle exploded on his shoulder, vibrating bone against muscle in a way that brought bile to the back of his throat. He could feel glass, small pieces, hanging from the side of his face. And there was an immense pain there. He slumped to the ground, removed his glove and ran his fingertips across the side of his face. His fingers came away warm and slick and the pieces of glass, the largest about the size of an aspirin, fell onto his coat. They were the smooth color of new raspberries.

14

"Hey it's Paul. Ronnie there?"

"Can you hold?" The voice on the other end of the phone was the classic example of bored obligation. He recognized it immediately.

More than a couple of minutes passed while Paul stood in the kitchen of his grandparents' home. His grandfather was gone, wasting the day somewhere at a gas station or outside a hardware store.

"Sir, are you there?"

"Yes, I'm here, Ed. Jesus. How long we worked together? Four years? Think you could at least call me Paul?" He stopped before saying anything else. No need taking out his anger on Ed, the receptionist.

"Okay, Mr. Shannon. Paul. Shit, this is weird. I'm patching you through to Ronnie. If he wants you treated like a leper, then he can do it. I wasn't hired to fire people."

It seemed his face had went numb. This despite his suspicions he was going to be fired. Confirmation from Ed was more than he could handle without some part of him going numb.

"Paul?"

"Ronnie, uh, listen, man."

"Save it, Paul. I don't know what you expect me

to say, but we gotta let you go. This thing's not up to me. But even if it were, I'd probably do the same thing. I know your dad died, and I know that sucks, but, hell, man, what do you expect?"

Paul was sure Ronnie was still talking, even after he cleared the front porch and was standing in front of Cramer's station. Ronnie might have continued talking even while Paul was walking into Cramer's station. Cramer was busy changing a balding tire. The replacement tire looked just as threadbare.

"Paul Shannon," Cramer said without looking up. "What can I do for you?"

"You can tell me one thing, Cramer."

"What's that, Paul?"

The feel of his knuckles slamming into Cramer's teeth hurt at first and then his hand was only tingling.

"Holy hell!" It was two of Cramer's dope-addled station attendants, Bill Jack and Caddy, calling out in unison. They dropped their tools on top of the car they were working on when Cramer staggered up from his crouched position.

Paul turned then and started back to his grandparents' house. It would be nearly a half hour before the police knocked on the door.

15

The first thing Paul thought about when they took him up the back entrance elevator was that he was about to use the bathroom. Instantly he realized the difference of being at home and about to piss and being in jail and about to piss.

So just like in first grade, Paul decided to ask.

"I need to use the bathroom," he said once they were at the front desk. The cop, who had been holding onto his upper bicep had moved across the open floor and was laughing with someone near what must have been a drop box of some kind.

"No you can't," an emotionless woman said from behind the counter. She was prepping a camera. "Stand over here in front of this blue square."

Mugshot.

Signature.

Holding cell.

No phone call, and his bladder hurt.

"There's a bathroom right over there," a guard wearing surgical gloves said. In his left hand was a mat, the kind kindergarten students used for nap time. It had seen better days. He tossed it in the middle of the holding cell, a ten foot by ten foot room, and snapped the gloves off. "There you go."

In the cell with him were eight other men. He counted from the corner of his eye while studying the toilet just off to the side of the far end of the room. These eight guys, one of whom was wearing only a pair of thin running shorts, feet black from pacing across the dirty floor, were going to watch him piss. There was just no way around it.

In plain view, with Blackfoot watching on, he pissed. For at least forty-five seconds that seemed more like ten minutes, he pissed with his hand guarding himself the best he could, considering a couple other inmates had joined Blackfoot in a rubbernecking routine that made his stomach curl. As he used the bathroom, Paul recalled that Larry hadn't been at his grandparents' house when he made it back from Hill's. Could be he already had a place to stay and had only dropped by to call on David. When he found out the bad news, he had decided to stay a couple nights. Could be he'd went back to wherever he'd come from. Paul suddenly felt ashamed for trying to pawn Larry off on Hill, for not standing up to his grandfather. He hoped Larry was still around. There was still the matter of offering proper thanks for what he'd done for him at Cramer's.

When he finished using the bathroom, Paul decided to initiate conversation. "Any of you guys got a phone call yet?" He was curious. He figured at least fifteen minutes had passed and still no mention of a call.

"Got a cigarette?" Blackfoot said.

"No I don't, man. Sorry."

"Dammit to HELL!"

Just like that the door to the cell swings open hard enough to make the single Plexiglas window breath inward.

"Got a problem, Sammy?" It was the guard with the gloves and the mat from earlier.

Paul decided to fade into a corner and wait for them to knock on the door and tell him he could make a phone call.

The guard, who looked about seventeen, gave Sammy Blackfoot two cigarettes to keep him quiet. After two more hours, Paul was beginning to think his phone call had been forgotten.

He got to his feet and felt his knees crack, bone against bone, bone pushing close to tendons, and pecked against the window with the back of his hand.

"Give it up, man." It was Blackfoot. Paul pretended not to hear him and knocked the glass again. "Did you hear me? I said it's pointless, pointless, pointless."

"Yeah."

"What'd you say?"

"Dammit to HELL!" Paul screamed. It was the best idea he'd had in a while.

The door swung open and immediately Blackfoot threw his hands in the air. "I don't know what he's screaming about," he said innocently.

Paul walked to the guard. "I've been in here for like five hours. I want my phone call."

He stood for a few seconds with the phone in his hand. The woman without emotion was licking her thumb and separating papers. She wore a dark blue uniform, neatly pressed, and her hair was pulled back in a bun so tight her eyes were left as two small slits. She didn't seem interested in rushing him, so he tried to take a minute and decide who to call. It might be a long time before he had the chance again. He knew his grandfather and the sheriff were close.

The phone rang five times before someone picked up. It was his grandmother.

"Mamaw, this is Paul."

"Paul, honey, where are you?"

"Listen, I'm in jail down here. Can you--"

"Lord, honey, don't tell your papaw."

Paul heard a loud click and then nothing. For about a full minute, he stood with the phone to his ear. When he finally took the phone away from his ear he instantly regretted it.

"Okay. Back in." The high strung desk clerk's voice was dry and deadpan.

"She hung up on me," Paul said in his most truthful but least whining voice.

A deputy jailer had him by the arm, pinching the muscle, moving him away from the desk and the clerk who hadn't looked away from her stack of papers.

He spent the next three hours in a corner of the holding cell watching a skinny man with dark hair holding his knees and rocking back and forth. He was facing the wall and whispering while he rocked. Two mats down from him, Blackfoot was talking about a dream he had. In the dream he had AIDS, he said. The cell door opened about four hours later.

"I need to make another phone call," Paul said quickly. The guard had two plates in his hand and was pulling a metal table with four others closer to him with the heel of one boot. Paul realized he sounded like a typical inmate, complaining and making demands, but he had no choice.

"I been in here, in this holding cell, for two-hundred and seventy-three days." It was Blackfoot leaning in close to his ear. "I never made one phone call. They put me in here to get me out of the general population. Can I have your coffee?"

The guard finished handing out the plates of food and then wandered over to Paul. "Won't need one. Somebody's out here gonna post your bond, I think."

In the holding cell there was a single window, and although it was large, it was rendered fairly useless to the inmates by a set of blinds that were apparently forever closed. No one had bothered to open them once in the several hours Paul had been pacing around the cell.

Now he rapped on the window, lightly at first, and then gaining steam with impatience. In the upper left corner, two of the blinds moved apart. Paul could see a small feminine finger and hooked thumb keeping them apart.

"Hey!"

The blinds opened for the first time since he had gotten there. Synthetic light poured through in bars of blue and pale yellow. Through the brightness, Paul made out a familiar face.

"Thank you, Jesus," he whispered against the blinds.

"You're welcome," Blackfoot answered.

16

On the ride from the jailhouse, Paul didn't speak to his uncle. It was clear Hill was put out. And it wasn't because he had dropped money on bailing him out. It was almost as if Hill could sense Paul's impending breakdown, or what he must have been sure would be Paul's breakdown. When they made it to the junkyard and were settled into Hill's trailer, Paul felt comfortable starting conversation.

"Don't suppose Larry's been here has he?" Paul asked after Hill switched off the air conditioning. The unit hung precariously from a window above his living room couch, scotched with a stumped two-by-four jammed into the bottom section of the window sill.

"I seen him around, up by Cramer's yesterday," Hill said. "He didn't say nothing, I didn't say nothing. I figure he's doing all right. Probably eating better than you have the past day."

Hill grinned for a second or two and then went serious. He swung his feet off the coffee table and leaned up from his seat.

"I managed a dismissal of charges with Judge Thomas, but you put me in a spot, that's for sure. Couldn't pull it off without easing into some kind of deal with Cramer. Turns out he just wanted to put a scare into you, get you to leave him alone. Guess he's joined everybody else in figuring that you're intending to stick around awhile."

"Cramer can kiss my ass," Paul said and eased onto the couch beside Hill. His head ached terribly and he smelled bad.

"Well that's good enough, I guess," Hill answered.

"How many times he dunned *you* for your dad's old bill? Two, three times? More? He can move to Michigan and die for all I care."

"Maybe leaving Red Knife would be a good thing for you," Hill said.

"I gotta go."

"That's what I'm saying."

"No, I mean I gotta head out."

Hill stood up quickly and held up one finger. He disappeared into the back of the trailer and came out with a photo album. "I reconsidered offering you the details about the tipple."

Handing the album over he said, "I would have brought it out a long time ago, but I just didn't see any reason for it. Plus, I wasn't sure your dad hadn't told you, or somebody else, for that matter. There was always the chance of that." He paused, thinking, "Either way, there it is."

The cover of the photo album was the color of mustard. Big round bulging spine and no description on the front. There was a buildup of permanent dust on both sides that didn't slide away when Paul rubbed the palm of his hand across it. Placing it on the kitchen island, he hooked his thumb under the cover and carefully let it fall open. The album seemed old and he wasn't surprised to find a black and white photograph on the first page.

The picture was of a smiling teenager. Clean skin, captivating smile full of broad white teeth. The teen's hair looked wet and was combed back from the forehead. He could still see the path the teeth of the comb left.

"You know who that is, don't you?" Hill said.

Until Hill asked, Paul would have been hard pressed to give an answer, but with a lead question like that, it became obvious.

"Dad?"

"Yep. Junior high. That was the year before the acne got hold of him. Damn that was bad. We hadn't even heard of laser surgery and here Dave was having it done on his face. Daddy thought they had poisoned him. Thought it had changed him because of how different he was later on."

"What're you doing with this anyway?"

There was a pop and then a quick dying away of fresh suds as Hill opened a beer. He shook his head a little and then took a drink. Paul could tell the beer was hot because there was no condensation on the outside of the can. Suddenly, with a picture of his smiling dad, a stranger to him, out in front of him he badly wanted a beer, cold or hot.

"Where'd you get that?"

"What, the album?"

"No, the beer. Well, and the album, yeah."

He tossed the photo album on the coffee table and walked three steps into the small kitchen. On the floor beside a garbage overfilled so that the sides heaved outward was a torn 10-pack carton. Inside there were three more Coors. He plucked one and turned back to Hill, who had finished his off.

"Yeah, you might need that." A certain gravity had taken over Hill's voice. He might have been easing his way into the ears of an unsure jury. "Thing is, what you're about to see. Hell, Paul, what you're about to see is what you're about to see, I guess. That's all."

Hill went silent while Paul stood in the door looking out on the junkyard. The dark purple of evening was finally starting to settle across the hills. Weak moonlight and starshine flinted off broken windshields. After three long drinks of beer, Paul twisted the tab off and tossed the can onto the heap rising up from the garbage can.

"Need to do some cleaning," Paul said. He settled himself over the album again.

"We found it under Dave's mattress. Look at it when you're ready," Hill said. "I'll be outside. Take as long as you want."

Paul watched Hill ease out the door, watched him as if his uncle might keep walking off into the night, out of sight and mind. In the new quiet of the trailer, he flipped the front page of the album and saw right away that a newspaper clipping covered the second page. The paper was brittle with age and had a large headline. In the headline was the word SEARCH. He closed the album.

Hill moved between a broken down Mercury and a Honda without wheels perched firmly atop a set of four cinder blocks. Soon the white of his shirt faded into the black of the metal landscape and became just another silent reflection of a star.

From the screen door Paul saw Hill moving around out by the junked cars. Pretty soon he stopped at a random vehicle and put his hands on his hips, popped the hood and started pushing and pulling at something out of sight deep into the workings of a motor that would probably never run again. The album was in his lap and he pulled the cover back again.

Hello, Dad.

Lively eyes, freshly combed hair. His black and white shirt mostly unbuttoned, revealing a crooked and imperfect black and white collarbone. A black and white nature scene had been dropped behind him. He turned the page and saw the newspaper clipping with the headline in all caps.

SEARCH FOR MISSING BOY CONTINUES.

And then another headline under that one.

Officials, Family Fear the Worst.

He read the story. It was vague in spots and clear in others, but the basics were that his father had once gone missing for just over three days. The date in the top right corner was June 14, 1966. The article said David Shannon had been missing for three days at that time. Paul thumbed through the pages until he came to the next story. Without reading the rest of this one, he thumbed quickly through several pages of the photo album. The final newspaper clipping included in the album came more quickly than he thought it would, and it wasn't the headline that caught his attention, but the feature picture that accompanied it. It was his dad, probably not more than two weeks after the yearbook picture was taken, the one where he looked fresh faced and ready to take on the world. But he now looked like an entirely different person. Two police officers flanked him. Their faces were solemn and serious. The photo caught his dad hanging his head, walking, it seemed, in such a way that the police were basically carrying him. In the background was only a hillside like any other hillside in the county. The headline was straight forward: RED KNIFE BOY FOUND.

Outside Hill stood up slowly from the spot he'd been leaning under the hood of a junked car. He reached behind him and pushed the balls of his wrists into the small of his back, let out a few grunts, and closed the hood. He could see Paul sitting on his couch through the living room window. He could almost see him drop the photo album beside him on the living room floor. Passing Paul on the way out he tried to pretend he didn't notice his nephew's face, how mashed up it looked with his peeled back lips and bloodshot eyes. And he didn't call after him when Paul popped off the porch and disappeared across the creek and into the darkness away from the trailer.

17

    Paul sat on the river bank with his knees pulled up to just below his chin. His dad squatted beside him, bent over an inflatable raft, inhaling and then exhaling in large bursts. The raft hardly moved, its thick blue and white wrinkles expanding only occasionally and then dying again, flat and collapsed.

    The raft was hardly a raft at all. It was more like a balloon. Along the river to the left of Paul and directly in front of his dad larger rafts negotiated the rapids, bought maybe in Wyoming and shipped here. They zipped past, full of laughing people, paddling people moving ahead while together he and his dad watched blue and white wrinkles grow large, disappear.

    When the job was complete, Paul stood beside the raft. Roughly six feet in length and about three feet wide, it would seat two people. There were no paddles, just the raft. After a minute to see that it didn't deflate, they pushed it to the edge of the water, scraping rocks and pebbles along the bottom. After the raft hit the water, held back with his dad's large grip, Paul thought then it would have been better if they had just picked the raft up. But he didn't say anything and instead eased carefully through the water and crawled into the raft in front of his dad, who had taken a seat in the back, one leg draped over the edge, anchoring the fifteen pound vessel with toes dug into the rocky riverbed.

No words, no conversation, as the two pushed ahead their combined weight and started across the water. Within seconds, a larger raft swept in from behind them carrying a man and two small boys, all wearing helmets, all wielding paddles, looking at Paul and his dad and the blue and white raft. They were laughing hard and they were laughing at Paul and his dad and the raft. They pushed ahead, and Paul couldn't see his dad behind him, but he knew what was in his eyes, blue determination.

The trip had been planned quickly after Paul returned from vacation with a set of cousins rarely heard from in Florida. His dad had sent Paul with his cousins, saying he couldn't afford a vacation, but if he wanted to go and stay for a couple weeks, it was fine by him. It had been a wonderful two weeks, and, when Paul returned, he spoke often of the things they had done. Fishing and strawberry picking and shooting basketball with the ocean twenty feet away. Two days after he returned, his dad bought this raft, and now here they were floating down the Big Sandy with the trees whipping past and the sky moving slower overhead and his dad tense and determined behind him.

The entire situation made Paul feel as if he couldn't gather air into his lugs. But, after a time, it was easy to forget with the way the river stretched out ahead of them, starting to turn from the muddy color that collected near the banks to the clear white-capped sections they were beginning to navigate. Paul didn't mention paddles, and saw no real reason to. His dad shifted from side to side, guiding the raft just to the left and right of rocks, hitting just the pocket of stream to keep them far enough away from the bank and moving ahead.

Further ahead, more rafts passed, canoes, families, friends, laughing. Pointing.

His dad bought the raft for ten dollars at a bait shop on the drive up. He was uncomfortable then, going into the shop and buying the raft. Paul could see it on his face. And he seemed uncomfortable now, spearing this way and that way, guiding the raft through the water. And before long, they were passing one of the custom-made rafts. No more laughing and pointing. Just stares. Paul didn't even look in their direction. He was focused on what was ahead, a clearing.

Other families rested in the clearing, backsides in the sand of the riverbank, their arms wrapped lazily around legs, heads hanging down, beaten by the short interval of rapids he and his dad had just cleared without paddles in a ten-dollar plastic raft found hanging above the display of nightcrawlers in a dusty cardboard box at Denver's Bait and Tackle Shop.

As the two swung into the clearing, Paul pulled at the sides, bringing the raft into a spot where the water was calm and tossed out, hanging the crook of his elbow onto the raft while his dad raised slowly and stepped into the water beside him. They walked onto the bank, pulling the raft behind them, and examined the men and boys drenched and banged up all along the bank. It was only then, when they were standing on the bank, Paul's dad stuck out his chest and nearly folded into the sand and rocks underfoot. He bent low, holding himself up with two large hands across his shaking kneecaps. Water dripped slowly from the tip of his nose and his hair hung in thick, black clumps over his eyes. And Paul stood beside him with his hand on his shoulder and then around his waist and then around him, holding him close enough to feel his heartbeat against his own chest.

"Let go of me," his dad said.

Paul stepped back slowly. "We made it," he said and tried a smile. He was still holding to his dad's elbow.

"Let go of me."

He let his arm drop and watched his father stalk off up the bank, past the fathers and sons without looking up. None of the sons and none of the fathers offered to help him deflate the raft and fold it under his arm. It was nearly dark before he finished, and he walked very slowly back to the car.

18

He was sure the old man he shared the not-taxi with on his way in was *the* John Harper. And he was pretty sure this man was there at the tipple that summer day when his dad's life changed. Somewhere deep within the well of himself he felt this to be true. The newspaper articles hadn't mentioned anything about the tipple, only his dad being held captive, and most of those details were stripped down to mostly law enforcement statements. It was fairly clear there was more to the whole thing than anybody was going to say publicly.

He was awake early enough that it would be another hour before sunrise. Larry was gone; that much was clear in the darkness. His dirty work boots that had been dropped during the night sometime beside the floor vent were gone, as were the two shirts and three pairs of pants he had bought a few days ago at the Dollar General. He might have gone to Hill's, but Paul doubted it. Larry Fenner had most likely felt William Shannon's weight on his shoulders, the weight that came from his eyes when you passed him and something was on his mind that dealt primarily with you. But it hardly mattered at this moment.

Now, at this moment, it was only John Harper,

son of George Harper; George Harper, a man so rich and so unwilling to talk about being rich that other men couldn't stand it. The myth and legend of this family was well learned and handed down in Red Knife. Paul knew the background as well as he knew that Herbert Hoover had caused the Depression, and through the same education, too. The school of William Shannon.

The Harpers were humble to their detriment, many said. It just ain't natural to keep so quiet about having so much, was the most common comment. But others chastised them for not giving to local charity drives and donation efforts. *Why, Clara Denton is the poorest thing since the bread line and she gives two dollars to anything that pops up. And two dollars ain't easy to come up with if you're Clara Denton. Them Harpers are tighter than bark on a tree.*

But the views held against the Harpers changed often. On days when the drives and charity seekers were out, it was condemnation all around, even for young John, who was then hardly more than a toddler. People called them Independents, registered against all parties. People called them Republicans, taking part in the hoarding away of their ample part of America's slimy dispersed wealth. More than anything people called them cheap and tight, but never to their faces, because soon the drives would settle back down and things were just things again. Before long it would be that about twelve percent of Red Knife's population was reminded that they were employees of the Harpers and that they had full medical coverage and a wage higher than that of the national average. They were invited to Christmas functions hosted by the Harpers and then views would change. But for some of the Harpers, it took a toll. Such was the case for John, so the education goes.

It began when George pulled his youngest son from school. The school principal, a round squat man named Benny Ward, who had a shiny face and very little hair and walked with the points of his scuffed shoes jutting outward, called on George the afternoon of the next school day. Ward had been informed that John was absent with no word from his mother or father.

Benny Ward went out there, but he wasn't too forceful. If he'd wanted to be forceful, he would have sent his director of pupil personnel officer, Jim Hanover, a man feared by every child in Red Knife. Jim was the man who would take you from your mommy and daddy and put you in a different house with different people who would make you go to school. Jim lived alone and was rarely seen outside. A pale man with a face frozen with seriousness and a weight from his duties, he told Cramer during an oil change once that he couldn't do it anymore. He said he couldn't keep taking children from their parents and placing them in foster homes. The story is that Cramer just kept draining the oil and never said a word. There was a reason he picked Cramer to tell, most people said. Cramer's oldest boy, Clay, was taken when he was four years old. Clay still lived around town, but never spoke to Cramer again.

But that morning it wasn't Jim who showed up at the Harper's farm, it was just Benny Ward wearing his tie too short and his pants hanging too far off his hips. George wasted no time in telling Ward that the reasons he pulled John from school were simple. He was being teased and tormented by the other students. They called John "Scroogy." Because of all the teasing, John's grades, which were once the top of his class, had dropped to the basement. It was homeschooling from here on out, George was said to have told Ward. And that was that. Those who remembered Scroogy from school were the rare few who had memories of him at all. It wasn't long after George pulled him from school that the home set up began to bleed over into everything else. John would take his math test and finish and then be told to go outside and play, but John never did. Instead he would sit by the window in the kitchen and watch the others.

That was when John Harper was eight years old. He wouldn't leave his house again as far as anyone knew. In late summer of 1967, a black car rolled away from the Harper's farm, which had been abandoned after the tragic end of the oldest son's death, and rolled away. Most knew it was weird John Harper they'd come after. He must have finally ended it. He was too young to have died of natural causes and a lonely suicide fit perfectly into the legend.

Around church gatherings and picnics, the town

whispered to one another that the end must have been a relief to the tormented man. He'd not been out of the house since his father pulled him from school, they said. He just sat watching by the kitchen window, mostly afraid.

19

Maysfield. About an hour drive from Red Knife.
There was no choice but for Paul to ask a Big Sandy
Transportation mini-bus to meet him at the IGA near
Long Fork for a pickup. Mini-buses and non-taxis;
public transportation in the hills was made of this kind
of tattered fabric. The transportation outfit was created
to get disabled people from place to place. But it
became a system anyone could use, as long as they
called and gave the mini-bus a route to pick them up.

"Wake up and be gettin' ready 'cause I ain't paid
to keep up with your business. Just get paid to drive.
You gotta tell me where you need off at."

The driver went quiet again. Paul had been
following a set of railroad tracks winding along beside
them in mostly a trance of sorts. It was nearly his stop.
He moved from his seat and started his way up the
aisle. Out the window he could see the railroad track
moving closer in front of them until before long they
were approaching the crossing where they had picked
up the old man.

"I need off at this crossing."

Paul loomed above the driver, nearly on top of
him. He felt wild. He smiled and had grabbed the top
of the seat so that he looked like some kind of bird, a

hawk maybe, spreading its wings. He lowered his head, looked out from pale blue eyes that gave him a hooded brow. The driver could see the man hadn't combed his hair because it was a pile of black corkscrews.

"At the crossing you say? That'll do." The driver turned back around and faced the road, away from the set of eyes still burning into his back.

Paul watched the not-taxi pull away and put his hand to his forehead and felt a cold sweat there. He felt dizzy and realized he hadn't changed shirts today, and maybe not yesterday either. He wasn't sure he'd done much of anything since reading the newspaper reports at Hill's that night. Full portions embedded into his memory came back to him as he made his way to the small walk bridge just down the hill.

"...Shannon's family did not comment on the incident, except to say they were pleased to have him home, and that he was recovering well, having suffered much physical strain during the ordeal...However, neighborhood friends of the Red Knife Junior High student, particularly those who were with him the day he disappeared, spoke briefly with members of the press shortly after the youth was discovered. On of those, David Shannon's brother, Hillman Shannon, said that he and his brother had been at Harper's Tipple with friends the day David Shannon went missing...Faculty at the school confirmed that David Shannon, Hillman Shannon and Thomas Spencer, of Pratt Hill Road, had apparently left school grounds just before the last hour of the day, having been marked as truant from their

seventh period classes...According to school records, only two other students were absent on the day Shannon went missing , one, Larry Fenner, whom Principal Ward said had a "history of absenteeism." Spencer and Fenner were not available for comment...With very few clues as to exactly how Shannon went missing, one thing authorities have had little trouble in understanding, however, is where David Shannon was eventually found. The particulars of that scene have not yet been released to the press, but sources close to the family have said the 12-year-old was nearly starved when found and had suffered from exhaustion, apparent shock and dehydration..."

Paul sat down on the bridge and put his head in his hands. Crossing his legs, he leaned over and listened to the water trickle beneath him. He had been there less than ten minutes when he felt a hand on his shoulder, soft and gentle, a nudge.

"Look here, son."

Paul turned quickly, startled despite the great gentleness of the touch and saw the old man, John Harper, standing on the bridge, tilted back on his heels with his hands in his pockets. He wore the same coat he had on the way to Lexington.

"You like this bridge do you?" the old man asked.

"No, not really." Paul didn't know what else to say. "Do you remember me? You said you were John Harper, do you remember?"

"Sure I remember."

"Well, are you John Harper? They told me you

were dead. Said you died." Paul's head had started to hurt and now he stood up slowly and ran his fingers through his hair. He could smell himself, rank and animal. He hadn't bathed in days.

"I'm John Harper, yes, and you're Paul Shannon, David Shannon's only son. Is that right?"

Paul didn't answer. Something was beginning to feel horribly wrong. While waiting for sight of Harper, he had taken out his wallet to get a clear picture of where he stood financially. The budget bonus he made just before leaving for the funeral was all but gone and the few dollars that were left would hardly pay for his ride back. He was broke, without a job, and in need of a shower, a shave, and a clean shirt. The wallet was still lying open on the bridge.

"Why don't you just ask what you came here to ask, Paul. Just ask, and I'll tell you."

Trickle. Trickle. Trickle.

"What happened to my dad?" The words came out with little fanfare. It was merely a verbal addition to a thought that had been circling within him since he was old enough to remember anything. "I know some of it, maybe enough, there's more there. I know it."

He had asked this question in the quiet dark more times than he had asked anything in his life. Saying them aloud now was only the logical next step. But in the past the question was mostly rhetorical; here there could be an answer. He felt sure there was an answer. "What happened to my dad?" he said again. A little louder this time.

20

"I have a plan," Dave said again.

He stood behind the others who had joined Larry along the tipple's outer catwalk. Each of them dangled their feet over the edge and took in small breaths of summer wind, hoping for something cooler might blow into the valley from a far off mountain top.

"You have a plan," Tommy mocked. He looked across the horizon. Fake puddles appeared along the scorched field. Except the puddles weren't water in his illusion. He imagined puddles of ice cold beer. Beer so cold it could bust a man's teeth.

Dave was standing behind them now, or more precisely, behind Larry. He dug his knuckles into the small of Larry's back and Larry winced and drew forward.

Hill looked around at Dave and drew his eyebrows down. At that moment, he looked more like their father than he ever would again. He pulled up Larry's shirt and made a sweeping motion with his hand at two snaking bruises in the area Dave had knuckled. Larry went motionless and kept looking forward, but his eyes were fixed now, not so dreamy. He breathed through his nose and although his dry and tiny lips were pulled together, Hill knew behind them were a set of clenched teeth.

Dave forced out an awkward half-apology and shrugged his shoulders at Hill. He sat down beside Larry and pointed to the pile of coal.

"Can you see that shining in the sun down there on that pile of coal, Larry?" The rest of the group strained to see what Dave was pointing out. "I do believe that is a something that, if not a crowbar, would definitely stand in quite nicely to pop this lock off, Master lock or not."

Silently, Larry stood up. He slumped toward the top of the ladder, but Dave caught up with him and put a gentle hand on his shoulder.

"Now I appreciate that gesture, Hoss, we all do, but they ain't a bit a use in you climbing all the way back down that thing when all you need to do is go off this side over here, plop down in that nice soft coal and bring that sucker right on up. That pile is easy twenty, twenty-five feet high, and when it sits like that for so long it breaks down and gets softer, weathered, that kind of thing."

"What?" It was Hill. He turned around from where he was sitting and put his eyebrows back in the same place as before.

"Don't give me that look, Hill. You know and I know — hell, maybe even Tommy knows — that coal, the way it's laying like that is just as soft as stack of dish rags. It ain't gonna' hurt Larry. Besides we all know too that he's just about the bravest and toughest guy in this bunch. You might not want to admit it, but it's true just the same." Dave was transformed to a pitch man, a traveling, one-man carnival barker. And he was throwing fastballs. "Who else would stand up at the Strand and sing 'The Old Gray Mule' with everybody there chomping on popcorn and waiting for the show? Who here would jump from the top of Clark's Tunnel into the back of a moving coal gon? We had to lift Dad's Chrysler and drive halfway across the state just to pick him up! And what was he doing when we picked him up?" Tommy shook his head, his eyes getting wider with every detail. Hill was now standing beside Larry and paying little attention. "He was taking bets with them locals on how many hot peppers he could eat in five minutes. He got through two and half jars with time to spare! Remember, Hill? We used the money for gas on the way back."

Hill nodded reflexively and then turned away.

"So then tell me, who else here is right for this job, this feat that will stand as a legend in this town?" His words were only partly sarcastic. The rest of the group could sense the realness beneath those words. The fact was simply that, although what Dave was saying was part of the routine meant to get Larry to do yet another crazy stunt, some of it, enough of it to make the rest remain quiet, was true. It would be Larry the towns people would remember years from now and tell their stories about. Their stories would not unfold the reality of what was his daily life, however, and that was his curse: to be remembered in the volumes of legend, yet not fully understood, not fully appreciated as a human being who could live through what was put upon him in his own backyard. It was these virtues for which Larry, had he been able and aware, would have chosen to be remembered. He found surviving his home life to be his greatest accomplishment, but the town would only remember hot peppers and coal gons. And tipples.

But, at least he would be remembered.

Hill and Tommy watched Larry inch forward toward the metal railing lining the catwalk. During most of Dave's speech about Larry's past exploits Larry had stood perfectly still. His posture was the same as he gripped the railing, arms trembling and shallow-breathing. And he continued to scan the horizon. The afternoon sun was already becoming mellow, less blinding white and more soft yellow, dull. But drops of sweat chased one another from the top and sides of Larry's burned head, the exact center of which had turned the color of ripe peaches and flaked and peeled away in spots.

"Nobody else, right?" Dave said.

"Why don't *you* go down and get something to open the box with?" Hill said. He had heard enough of his brother's speeches to not fall into the kind of trance others did. And he knew right and wrong enough to not get caught up in pushing Larry to do something deadly dangerous.

"Forget it, then, I'll do it," Dave said and turned and was about to head down the ladder when a loose section of catwalk shifted beneath his feet and popped him four inches into the air.

He turned in time to see Tommy, who had kept his seat along the edge of the catwalk, spring into the air and then land roughly back into place, his mouth gaping open and his head bent, watching Larry drop through the air.

"Christ Almighty!" Tommy yelled out.

Larry dropped feet first, no movement. No flailing about or arms spinning for balance. His legs were motionless, and as he turned in the air like a suspended needle the boys could clearly see his face. He could have been asleep. That was Hill's first thought as Larry tilted skyward and came into view. His eyes were open but looked absent and bored. He crossed his hands over his chest and then, just as he was about to land in the pile of coal, instant realization seemed to set in. He seemed to understand what he had done and pushed his hands toward the ground, useless and futile.

Even from the hundred or so feet above, the boys could hear the sound of Larry landing in the coal. He hit about four feet from the center, feet first, and the sound was like a slab of raw meat being thrown carelessly onto a stainless steel counter. His body shifted in speed so suddenly that his neck snapped forward violently and as Tommy noticed what happened to his legs on impact, he leaned over the opposite side of the railing and spat green and yellow vomit.

Larry's legs folded together like twin

switchblades, bloating and creasing as they went. Both knees of his pants spread dark crimson just before he tilted to the left and flopped lifelessly to the ground. The sound of his voice booming through the valley was horrible. Tortured and full of regret and confusion

Below, Larry's world shifted and swirled. He landed roughly in a field of blooming dandelions and now he could only see patches, small circles of yellow, swaying in front of his eyes. He could smell the warm earth beneath his face and could feel pinpricks of coal disrupted and now falling back onto his left cheek from the force of each scream he could manage. He tried to move, but his legs and hips were numb. He searched to feel the rounded proof that his hips were still there and realized his torso and much of his chest was also numb. In the seconds he lay motionless in the grass he remembered his mother explaining to him how death worked over a dying body. He remembered clearly and with growing horror her explaining that death would take a body slowly, first the toes and then the feet. The legs would follow and death would work its way up the body that way. Things would become cold, she said, and then finally death would clutch his heart and take the soul.

Larry sat still now, no longer screaming, and waited for death to take his soul, understanding why his body, crumpled and broken, would be useless for any purpose. The soul would be the only thing left for use. Before the dancing circles of yellow melted and went dark, Larry's last thought was that his mother would just now be starting to peel potatoes for dinner, stripping away the skins while his father gathered them for the fire. He would just now be tossing the skins into the fire, Larry figured, watching them curl and waiting for his supper.

21

"I was at the kitchen window when he jumped. By God, I didn't think he was going to do it, but I could tell he was going to do something. I just didn't think he was going to do that, jump like that." The old man sucked wind between his teeth and looked at the nearby hills.

Paul watched the twisting waters of the stream. A clump of orange and brown leaves clogged one section and developed a natural dam about the size of a person's fist. He resisted the urge to toss a nearby pebble into the water to break it loose.

"What'd you do after he jumped? I mean what happened?"

John Harper fell into silence for nearly a full minute, weighted down by a conversation he never expected to have, had, in fact, never spoken of until this second.

"Your dad, David, he ran down the tipple ladder. I mean he might as well ran down. He hardly even bothered to grab on. He just dropped them rungs in big steps and was on the ground in no time. The others, I recognized your uncle Hill, the one who they say went on to law school or some such thing, were a little ways behind, but rushing pretty good too. The other boy took off running and was gone in no time across the field and I couldn't see him anymore. Hill started up to your dad and Larry and then turned around and, just like the other one, was gone across the field. He kept looking back, but he kept running." The old man stopped and shifted from one foot to another. A cool wind carried the scent of manure, tossing it around in the valley. "Your dad wasn't a very big boy when he was that age. I remember he was really kind of underweight with these big ears that stuck out and caused him to look damn near top heavy. But he pulled that big rascal up from the ground." Harper stopped again and lowered his head. He shivered through his shoulders and out through his arms and hands, which were stuffed deep into his pockets. "He pulled Larry up. Took him under the arms and lifted and when he did that boy's poor legs just hung there like bloody dish rags. Jesus and the way he hollered out. I can still hear him."

Paul seemed to jerk inside his own skin. "But you just sat there in that kitchen didn't you and watched him." His nostrils flared, whistling sounds across the two or three feet of space between them.

"I did," Harper said calmly. "I sit right there and watched him heft that boy onto his back and start dragging him. Is that what you want to hear, that I couldn't get myself to run out to that field to just lend a helping hand?"

Paul stood up and looked at Harper. "Yeah, I

guess so."

Harper laughed. "Well, I didn't. Not just then. I didn't figure your dad could drag that big old boy more than ten feet without falling. But that wasn't the case. That wasn't the case at all."

Harper turned and walked away from the bridge. He could hear Paul trudging behind him, labored breathing and stomping across the ground. Too much time in the city, he figured, not enough time in the hills. Not enough time lately off-balance with his ankles turned over to call himself a hillbilly.

"Where we going, to your house?"

"Absolutely. I live just over that ridge there. You'll see when we get there that I can see the bridge from the front porch. Saw you get out of the taxi, in fact.."

"Not-taxi."

"Pardon?"

"Nevermind," Paul said, and when Harper went quiet added: "Well, can you talk and walk at the same time?"

At about that time Paul caught a small tree branch before stumbling. He threw his arms out in front of him and stopped to put his hands on his knees. "Shit I'm out of practice for hill-climbing."

"You sure are if you think this is hill-climbing," Harper said, and pointed up and to his left. "Here we are."

Topping off along the ridge was a squat house that looked to have about four or five rooms at best.

The sides were peeling and flakes of brown, maybe red paint hung to porous boards and dirty white window sills. The highlight was a front porch, newly built, it seemed, new wood, a dramatic contrast to the dullness of the rest of the house. On the porch, sitting as still as the house itself, was a woman in a flower dress holding a cup in her hand. She didn't wave when she noticed them. Her eyes, obviously a very light color of blue, were noticeable even from the distance where Paul and Harper were making their way up the tiny hill. They seared across the distance between them, cutting down from where she sat like blue spotlights. If Paul would have been asked to describe her later, he would have talked about Indian squaws and portraits that seemed to have moving eyes that followed you across rooms. But just this minute, clutching the edge of the porch and hearing that sound like a band student bound for a failing grade seeping from his throat, Paul only cared for hearing Harper out and then getting back to the bridge. He wasn't sure how much time had passed since the bus had dropped him off and the sky was starting to turn the color of a week-old bruise.

"Let's go inside, have a seat," John said. He might have picked up on Paul's great urge to move along. "You'll want to take your time and hear this, Paul."

Harper's wife was still in her rocking chair. She hadn't looked at the two of them since she spotted them coming up the hill. In her lap was a mess of beans. She was grabbing three at a time and breaking, each movement punctuated with the snap of cold vegetables that have been stored since growing season. She took no notice, only looked out over the field into the trees beyond.

Paul looked at her and for just an instant he thought he saw her move her eyes toward him, just briefly. "She know?" Paul asked.

"Sure. Augustine's my wife. A wife knows everything."

Her eyes had said just hang in there for a minute and listen, you'll want to hear this.

Paul made his way up the high set of steps and followed Harper into the house. Inside, the conditions the two were living in had to have been a stark contrast to the life John Harper must have grown used to being raised by the richest family in three counties. The living room was adequate enough with two couches and a fireplace. In the left corner of the room was a table with a very old lamp placed in its middle. A dusty brown cord connected it to an outlet in the wall that itself barely hung to its fixings. It looked like it had been gutted one too many times during a shoddy attempt to rewire the house.

The windows were open letting cool fall air move freely through the house, but it wasn't chilly inside. Instead, it was stuffy, like maybe the night before Harper and his wife had to light the fire to knock off the chill. Paul looked into the fireplace and saw gray ashes and caught the faint scent of smoke and dowsed wood.

Harper moved through the living room with ease, steps he had taken many times over the years. His walk was content, slow and deliberate, not so much with purpose as with a sense that there was no real place to be going and that that was perfectly fine.

Paul followed him into a very small kitchen area. A miniature stove sat inside a miniature two compartment sink. Above the sink was a plaque that read, *May you be in Heaven a half hour before the Devil even knows you're dead.* Harper took a seat at a table less than half the size of the one in the living room and plopped his elbows up. After a long breath, he started right in.

"When Larry jumped off that tipple and your daddy got down there and picked him up, I thought he wouldn't be able to drag that boy but about ten feet. When he disappeared out of sight, which was about a hundred feet, I actually went outside for a better look." Harper stopped here, looked at Paul, and then examined his hands for a beat or two. They were shaking. "Well, anyway, I went outside. It was so bright, I remember, but I started across the field and then started going faster and faster. Before long I caught up with your dad, still dragging Fenner. That boy's legs was busted up horrible. His pants were just soaked and he wasn't hollering or groaning anymore. It looked like he'd just went on out, passed out there on his back. I stayed close, but not too close, and I know what you're sittin' over there figuring on, but just put it out of your mind. They wasn't a way in the world I could help that boy. Actually talking to somebody just couldn't happen, no matter what was going on. Stepping outside at all was some kind of miracle. Or adrenaline or some such thing."

"Mr. Harper. John. I respect all that, I really do, and I thank you for talking with me, but I need to know what happened, so can we just--"

Harper stood up and put his hands on his sides, pushing his chest out just a bit. "That's exactly what I'm doing here, young man. There's things that ain't easy for people in this world and what happened to me that day saved my life. I felt it important enough to make mention of, don't you agree?"

Paul nodded. His head throbbed and a five-column front page feature picture from the Maysville News-Record kept floating in front of him, a picture of his dad with cops holding him up as he tried to walk. So skinny, his face a sunken crater of pain and, just beneath that, the exhausted joy of the near dead breathing again. The look of life renewed and misery completed. The image replaced in his memory the black and white image of his father sitting for his school picture, hair neatly parted with a bright smile, playful, probably joking with the photographer and laughing. A laughing smile.

Harper sat back down and looked across the small area of the kitchen. "Your dad dragged that boy all the way back to Joe Fenner's. I followed them all the way and tucked in behind the old barn out from that front yard dirt garden of Joe's. I ran up to the window after they went inside and saw Joe's face when your dad pulled Larry up from the floor and pointed at his legs. He was talking fast, that's for sure." Harper stopped. Across the old wood of the table his hands lay one on top of another shaking.

"What?"

"This ain't something's gonna be easy to hear, probably."

"I figured about as much."

"Joe Fenner hit your daddy with a closed fist in the face harder than I've ever seen anybody hit to this day."

The air squeezed from Paul's chest and little to nothing moved through his throat. He heard himself sputtering conversational vowel sounds, grunts and affirmatives, but he couldn't get hold of them and put them together to make any sense.

Harper sat still as stone, sometimes looking at Paul, other times looking away. He didn't' look surprised; he looked like he didn't know what to do with his eyes.

"He hit Dad? I don't understand."

"Does anybody? You knew about Joe Fenner. Does anybody ever understand anything about a man like that? He raped his wife more times than he kissed her, beat a stable of horses to death and made his boy work in their place. He hit your daddy, and that's not all. I left after he put him in the back tool shed."

22

By the time Dave made it down the ladder to Larry laying crumpled at the foot of the tipple, his hands were scalded from the blasting heat of the metal rungs.

He had watched a boy get his teeth busted out playing basketball two years before. The boy, a freshman at the high school named Barry, was known for fighting and known for hunting for a good one from time to time. One day during lunch Barry trotted with his chest stuck out onto the court where the seniors were playing, skinny and a foot shorter than any one of them. They laughed and then shot for teams. Barry was last and got stuck with Simon Cook, the senior pack leader, the Alpha and Omega of the high school world.

First possession Barry barked at Simon for having girl hands when the big boy dropped a looping pass along the sideline. Simon didn't' waste time. He hadn't said a thing to Barry. After the comment, he took off after the ball that had started rolling toward the school building, grabbing it up quickly and stalking back to where Barry stood with his hands on his hips. Two boys who had been standing behind Barry hooked his arms and pulled backwards onto the ground. There on the hot blacktop of the court, they took Barry's head in their hands and pulled it back onto the ground while Simon, smiling, pulled up over top of him with the ball held in both hands. He then raised it into the air, blotting out the sun and shading Barry's face, and brought it down into Barry's mouth. There was a wet crunch and choking. Somebody ran for the teachers and Barry's face was shooting blood like a fountain. When the teachers came, one of the first things they did, before even picking Barry up from the ground, was to pluck two small teeth from the side of his face. They were hanging on, stuck in the thick red blood gushing from Barry's mouth. Barry lost all his teeth that day with one well-placed hit. Dave had thought it would be the most blood he would ever see.

Larry was so much worse. He lay face down in the grass less than three feet from the pile of coal, breathing in strange fits against the ground. His back and legs shook and jerked radically, as if seizing. At the end of one outstretched arm, Dave could see he had grabbed the grass and some wild flowers were in his left hand and clutched hard, hard enough that the knuckles of his hand were white. He wasn't moving otherwise, and, other than the breathing, made no other sounds.

"Larry, Larry. Hey, Larry." Dave rushed up to him and took him under the arms. The weight was incredible. He had heard stories from an older cousin about training to be a state trooper. He said the worst thing during boot camp was something he called the "dummy drag" where the trainees would have to run an obstacle course carrying a dummy that was fixed up with the same proportions of a real person, two-hundred pounds plus. Larry Fenner easily weighed as much, and with him limp and completely helpless it was more burdened weight than anything else. That's what his cousin said it was called, burdened weight. It's how much something weighs that's basically not helping you along at all. Like a dead person, or somebody who just jumped off a tipple on to a pile of coal.

Dave thought Larry might scream when he lifted him up, but he only breathed and choked more. Larry closed his eyes when Dave turned a one-eighty and started in the opposite direction. His bones snapped under the skin and he smelled piss and shit and the coppery scent of blood. He tried not to breathe except in large gulps through his mouth while he dragged Larry across the field and along the side of the road leading to Fenner's farm. If he could just make it to the farm and get Larry to his folks, they could get him to a hospital.

Joe Fenner leaned across the railing of his front porch. The sunlight caught in his eyes and he squinted. When he did, the skin that had been stretched tight and slick across his forehead crumpled up and created deep grooves. He saw two figures at the end of the garden and rapped his cane on the flooring of his porch.

"Who is it!"

Dave tried to push out a response, but only

managed a small whisper, lost against Larry's slumped shoulder.

"I said who the hell's there!" Joe Fenner looked closer and made out Larry through the early twilight. "Goddamn. Larry."

"He's hurt, Mr. Fenner," Dave was able to say after meeting Joe at the foot of the steps.

With an incredible and hidden strength, Joe Fenner grabbed his boy under the arms, his own arms bulging with small but hard muscles and rope-thick veins, and tossed him onto the porch with a thud that shook the porch railings. Larry, who hadn't made a sound since yelling after the fall, now groaned and started crying, quietly, almost to himself.

"Mr. Fenner, Larry fell off the tipple out at—"

His fist felt good hitting the Shannon boy's cheek. The punch knocked him right out; he could tell by the way the boy's legs went out from under him and how his body curved to the side on the way down. He craned his leathered neck around and searched the doorway. "Clara, come out here and get this boy. Splint up his legs. He's broke 'em all to shit. Maybe his hips too."

Stepping around a puddle of blood collecting at the cuff of Larry's pants, Joe scooped Dave easily onto his shoulder and started around the side of the house, spitting absently on the horse as he did. It whined and turned its big glossy eyes, tossed its head and backed up into its makeshift stall. The Shannon boy didn't weigh more than a hundred and thirty pounds at the most, Joe figured. He could hardly even feel him on his shoulder as he turned the corner of the house and started toward the tool shed. It was a squat shack about six feet by five feet just off from the garden and not used much during the hottest part of summer. When he tossed the latch and let the door swing outward on its hinges, a wall of heat washed over him and he could feel the boy take a deep pitiful breath.

"In you go, you little prick." And then with timed heaves: "In...you...go!"

Dave hit the cracked dirt of the shed floor flat on his back. The air pushed out of him as he opened his eyes. The skin along the side of his face became tight the way the skin on his shoulders felt after a good sunburn had set in. The hot air inside the shed was making his lungs feel swollen and bloated, scorched and ready to collapse. And the pain from the left side of his face was getting worse as he came to more and more.

Dave couldn't tell when he was fully aware of things around him. His head throbbed and ached as if it was filled with spurred ball bearings and his mouth felt thick. Carefully he pushed himself to a sitting position in the middle of the shed and tried to examine the darkness around him. Through the clapboard sides of the shed there was the purple light of early evening spearing into the shed giving him just enough light to make out a storage shelf. Beside that a saw hung from a nail and then below that a can of what must have been gasoline. Other than this, he couldn't make out much else. He jumped to his feet, staggered against the side of the building, and felt pain shoot through his face and into his neck. He threw himself against what he figured to be the door of the shed.

"Hey!" His voice sounded foreign, like someone else's, like the voices of the people being chased in the movies he and Hill sometimes watched at Plaza Movies. The people who were about to be knifed and buried in the garden. "Hey! Hey! Hey!" He slammed the palms of his hands against the rough lumber door until they were sore and bleeding just enough to make his hands slick and stinging from the sweat. And then, very faintly, he heard someone say Joe Fenner's name.

"Hey! Let me out!" He fell to his knees, listening for the voice again, the voice of a woman he was almost sure, maybe Larry's mother. Where was Larry? "Please let me out...Larry needs to go to the hospital. Larry's legs are gone...Larry needs legs..." He shifted back onto his hands and felt the hard wood of the shed cut him off from falling. The purple spears of light were quickly vanishing and he felt sick. His body was covered in sweat and blood that ran from a large cut across his swollen cheekbone. He blinked sweat away and in that second, in the time it took him to shutter his eyelid, the shed was completely dark, encased in a darkness so vast and so absent of hope that he slid down the wall and landed in a heap on the ground. He could smell the gas just to his left. He could hear footsteps in the house outside and he could hear his heart beating hard inside his chest. He could hear his fear moving inside him like mercury, deadening him to thought and emotion, making him slip into a scorched, painful sleep.

In his sleep Dave muttered about hospitals and legs and gas and fire and tools and when he woke a half hour later, he felt stronger and started running his outstretched hands across the slick and warm packed earth of the tool shed floor, hunting for a tool—a crowbar or a lug wrench. Within minutes he stopped and slumped forward, let out a long sigh, and feathered his fingers to the side of his face. It was sore and swollen, the skin tighter now, but he had broken bones before, and he wasn't convinced that his cheek was broken. It wasn't numb. It was in flames.

Once he was able, he got slowly to his feet and dumped his head against his chest. When he did, the pain in his cheek exploded into a brighter pain for a couple of seconds and then eased off again. He could smell the gasoline and the shit just beneath that, a deep scent of manure.

More or less blind in the dark, the sounds from the house, the hurried sounds of people dealing with an emergency and fighting while doing it, had subsided. Dave pushed his arm out into the blackness and found the adjacent wall and worked his way to where he remembered the door was located. About midway down the door, running his fingers along the splintery surface, he found a bored out hole not big enough to squeeze his fist through. Dropping to his knees, he pushed his eye as close to the hole as his burning cheekbone would allow and made out a small light floating in the circle of black. As it grew larger and closer, the dead sound of footsteps became clear and he backed up on his hands, expecting the door to swing open. But instead, a voice, low and quiet, poured through the hole in the door.

"Dave." A whisper, low and scared, trembling butterfly wings against the outside of the door.

Dave moved quickly across the floor and slammed against the door. The clapboard tool shack creaked and rocked slightly to the left when he did. A lantern tilted back and forth through the opening. "Let me out, please, let me out, please."

"Shhh, now be quiet, little Shannon. I can't let you outta there, boy. Don't you understand that? My boy's a laying in there with his legs needing chopped off and I can't take him to no hospital. Joe won't allow it. Just wanted you to know about Larry." She stopped talking and the blackness returned as the lantern moved out of sight. He wanted nothing more than to just cry right there on the dirt floor. "Joe's mean, but you deserve this, you know that. You deserve whatever evil he pushes on you, little Shannon."

The door to the shed slammed forward violently. For a few seconds there was silence, but this was followed by open weeping and footsteps returning to the porch and into the house.The last of those sounds had just started to grow faint when another set of
footsteps hit the back porch. Boots, hard against wood.

Intent.

"Heya there, boy!" This was yelled well before anyone reached the tool shed, and then Joe Fenner was at the door. "I got this board over the door here and you ain't gettin' out. You hear me? I'm keeping you, boy. I gonna take your legs because you took my boy's legs. He told me what happened. Said you boys put him up to dropping off that fucking tipple out at Harper's. You gonna pay for that. You gonna pay hard. The hardest." His voice had became a hiss, a snake crawling toward the door.

It occurred to Dave with perfect clarity that Joe Fenner was lying. Larry would never have said that, even though it was closer to what could be the truth than anything else. Larry would have just said nothing like he always did after Joe gave him a good beating for nothing. Beat for nothing; says nothing. That was Larry. He was not a rat. Not even when it might help him in some way.

Dave didn't ask why they were going to keep Larry in his house instead of taking him to a hospital. He wanted to, but instead he just pictured Larry there inside the house, maybe strapped to the bed, crying and tears rolling down his face, probably with a cup of hard liquor on the table beside him. Take a drink of this, boy. It'll take the pain away. But it wouldn't ever take away the pain. They would have to take him to the hospital soon and Dave knew it.

At an incredibly deep level, Dave understood, after having been in the shed just a few hours, that this would be his opportunity to get away, whenever they left for the hospital. They would have to. They couldn't take care of him here with that kind of injury. And then, perfectly on cue, Joe Fenner hissed again through the hole in the door.

"You think we're taking him someplace, leaving you here on your own in that hot old shed without water and food, you got another thing comin', Shannon. We ain't goin' nowhere. We're going to stay right here. She's gonna take care of him—" He hooked his thumb toward the house, "—and I'm gonna take care of you."

Food and water. Dave hadn't even thought about food and water, and right now it wasn't food that was on his mind, but water, something wet. The heat inside the shed became more and more of an issue with each passing minute. The pain in his cheek subsided and the dryness in his throat grew worse. How long could a person go without drinking water? His grandmother, who lived to be one-hundred and three before dying in a nursing home, told him a person couldn't go more than a day. They'd die, she said, as sure as a flower will wilt into the ground and away from the sun. She had told him just like that, with the wilting and the sun and the dying.

Time lost value to Dave. He sat on the ground in the dark. His throat hurt and his cheek was no longer throbbing, but the pain was still there. From time to time, he put his fingers carefully to the side of his face, pushed and tested the pain. It was something to do.

Joe Fenner brought a pan of water from a long dormant dog house at some point, just as it was getting dark, and placed it about a foot from the door of the shed. Dave crouched close to the dirt floor and made out the dull silver pan, a baking pan that looked like the one his mother made biscuits in most mornings. He could just make it out. What could have been an hour earlier or ten minutes earlier, a skinny and beaten brown and yellow cat slinked past and stopped for a drink. He remembered the sound its tongue made while darting in and out of the water. The sound kept going through his head. He swallowed hard, felt and heard a quick click move across his Adam's apple and tried not to think about his parents looking for him. Surely one of the boys had told what happened. But maybe they hadn't. Maybe they were too scared and thought maybe he was hiding out and scared too. The last seemed the more likely possibility and the truth of this forced a sinking inside his chest.

Again, in his defeated way, he fell backward into the slatted walls of the shed. There was a snap and crack somewhere in the dark that startled him until he realized the sound came from the wall itself. Joe Fenner built the shed roughly but solid; a carpenter as well as a farmer, Joe made a small living at both. But the shed was old and the wood was dried and beaten from weather and age. Dave leaned back again, hard and fast and heard the crack again. It reverberated across the Fenner's back yard, interrupted the very early morning sounds from creatures waking up in the hills just beyond. Though risky, he kept shoving against the wall and made some progress. A couple more hits and he might knock a board loose and that would give him enough room to hook his fingers, get a good hold, and pull the rest of the rest out of the way. He'd get out one board at a time.

When the first board gave against his back, part of his side pushed through. He felt a stout piece of splintered wood pop through the skin along his side. He fell sideways onto the floor and clutched at himself with both hands. He pulled his shirt up and ran his hand across his side. He felt blood spreading under his palm, but no splinter, no piece of wood jutting out. Immediately, he started tugging at the boards on both sides of the new opening. He was gaining strength with each half inch of progress he made. The purple light of twilight was returning again, this time with the sunrise.

From a distance, he couldn't exactly tell how far, a rooster crowed a shrieking blast across the silence. Dave stopped then and sat down, breathing hard clicks into the muggy air. The screen door from the back porch creaked and smacked back into place. He closed his eyes and opened them when he heard the board across the door of the shed popped loose from its place. The first thing he saw was Joe Fenner's eyes through the new opening. The eyes rested on Dave, deadpan and motionless, and then darted around wildly to examine the progress he'd made on the wall of the shed.

"Tell you what," Joe said. "I'm gonna step over here and throw this old shed latch and I want you to try to jump out of there. I'm gonna leave the door open so you can do that very thing, cause then I'm gonna kill you quick. That's what she says I should do." He hooked his thumb again toward the house the way he had the evening before. "So you just take a run for it when I go over there if you want. I'll kill you quick and then she'll be satisfied. You don't' take a run for it when I leave this door open, then I'm gonna make it slow and she won't like it, and if Momma's not happy ain't nobody happy."

He rubbed the gray stubble along his cheek, smiled, and then laughed a little. It was morning and he was feeling better it seemed. Larry must have been asleep and resting and, impossibly, it seemed things might somehow be okay. "Naw, I guess I'll lock it. I'd like it to be good and slow. I'll just tell her you were too scared to make a run for it. How's that sound? Fine. Yes, fine I think. Just fine."

He popped the door closed and stomped across the yard and picked up a fresh two-by-four. He stomped his way back to the shed and flung the shed door wide. Joe spun the board sideways in both hands and brought it down on Dave's kneecap. Like flashes of lightning, three more hits came across his legs and then a fourth across his left shoulder.

The pain shocked him in such a way that he could only spread his mouth wide and wheeze. He had once closed his finger in a car door while pumping gas for his dad. The door closed perfectly without a hitch. He stood a couple seconds looking at his hand caught in the door and thought how strange it was that the door had been able to close over his finger and then tapped calmly on the window and asked his mother to open the door. It hurt more later than when it happened. He figured this would be the same.

"Yeah, yeah, yeah." Joe's voice was whisper-crazed and mad and then the old man's hands were grasping the sides of Dave's head. "See on that wall, scratched right above where you been peckin' and pullin' like some old woodpecker? You see that, them scratches there? That'll help you keep up with the day. Just count 'em down." He pushed Dave back onto the floor and turned to leave, kicking the pan of water over as he did. He turned back around and ran his fingers through his hair, waking up more now, ready to face the day. "That's the way Larry got through it, I reckon. He's the one put most of 'em there. At least half."

Just before Joe Fenner closed the door, Dave had a second to look up again at the marks scratched into the boards. Jagged scratches made with a nail maybe or something sharp. Three rows of about ten or so it looked like.

In the dimness, Dave got to his feet and touched the wall. He ran his fingers over the dug out lines and thought of his face and how it was probably swelled. Then he thought of Larry standing where he was now, raking and scratching to make his marks.

156

Probably crying. Probably hurting. Probably scared.

He finished counting the marks.

Twenty-seven deeply grooved slashes.

On the porch Joe Fenner shook caked mud from his boots and slipped them from his feet. He bent slowly, plucked them up with three fingers, and placed them beside the door. Inside he removed his coat. Underneath was a set of long pajamas the color of freshly unearthed bone. He scratched at these as he went through the kitchen and into the bedroom.

Clara was still asleep, or if she wasn't she pretended to be. He would be hungry soon and if she continued to pretend then, he'd let her know it. For now he walked loudly to the side of the bed, sat down roughly, and dusted the dirt picked up from the hardwood floors from the bottom of his feet. He crashed back onto the pillow and steadied his breathing.

He stayed in bed for about five minutes, occasionally leaning over to pull the curtains on the bedroom window and look out at the shed. Finally he groped around for his watch on the nightstand, turned it into the weak morning light through the pulled back curtains and got out of bed. He tucked his feet into a pair of dusty brown wingtips without strings and clapped through the short hallway. Raking like an animal grooming he pushed his fingers through his hair and stopped at the doorway of Larry's bedroom.

Larry's labored and beaten snoring and sucking sounds filled the room. Short breaths and long grunts, and then the broken sucks of someone trying to breath without moving their ribs. Larry squinted his eyelids and tried to make out his father in the doorway, hoping to get a read on his mood. His arms were pinned at his sides and his legs bulged from under the covers, box-like from the splints. At last, Joe stopped looking at Larry and went to the bedroom window to peel the curtain back in his casual kind of way.

"Daddy?"

In the bed, Larry's arms were now folded across his chest. The fingers, long and trembling, were moving up and down like a piano player, up and down along the lining of the covers. Joe didn't say anything but took one step toward the bed.

"Daddy," Larry said again.

Joe pulled the covers back from Larry's legs and felt wind catch inside his throat. He pushed it up and out through his nose with a snort, then sniffed and looked away.

The legs looked bad. In some places there was black splotches and they were swelled, had swelled through the night, so bad that the bean rope he had tied the splints together with were drawn tight and cutting into all the bloat. The legs were going to have to be fixed and this just was not going to do.

"Can you cover me back up, Daddy? With the yeller flowers, can you cover me back up?"

Gibberish. Joe moved absently and tossed the

cover back over the legs. "They'll have to run some rods through them things, ain't no doubt."

He left the bedroom with Larry saying "Daddy" over and over again and heard his son start to cry when he passed through the doorway. Back in the living room Joe paused at a vanity mirror and pushed his hair back. With the tonic from the morning before still holding, it only took a few swipes to get things in place and then he went back to his bedroom. Clara had turned over on her back. She never slept on her back. She was pretending for sure.

"I'm gonna have to take him to the hospital," he said, going to a tiny closet at the foot of the bed. "Something ain't right and I know you're gonna want me to take him anyway if you get a look at the legs." He pulled on a pair of dark work pants and buttoned them with two long fingers while reaching back into the closet for a brown work shirt.

Clara swung her legs over the side of the bed and pulled her hair back as an afterthought. She hooked a plastic clamp to it so that it bounced up from the top of her head. Leaning over, she tossed back the curtain and eyeballed the shed.

"I wanted you to take him soon as he got here," she said, looking down at her feet, rubbing them together and feeling the hard calluses on the insides of both her big toes.

"You'll have to watch close while I'm gone," Joe said. "I know it's what that boy's been waiting on out there. For us to leave so he can bust through that shit shack."

Clara Fenner stood up slowly from the bed and stretched her plump fingers outwards toward the walls of the bedroom. Loose skin swayed from her arms. "You go on and take Larry on to the doctor. Everything'll be okay here."

Joe's face stoned over, serious and demanding. "Don't let that boy out. You hear me?"

"You think I lost my mind in my sleep last night? I ain't lettin' him go nowhere."

"You ain't lettin' him go nowhere," Joe repeated. "That right? You goddamn right you ain't lettin' him go nowhere. You goddamn right."

Dave stretched out across the dirt. Lifting his shirt, he flattened out so the cool packed ground touched as much of his skin as possible. But it wouldn't stay cool for long. He could already smell the heat working on the sides of the shed, the smell of hot wood heating up in the sun.

Earlier a door had slammed on the house and the sound of an old car cranking to life had filled the valley. The sound of footsteps across the porch followed that. Out the hole where a knob should have been he saw Joe Fenner stomp into the house. Soon he reappeared carrying Larry by hooking his forearms up and under the pits, clenching in on Larry's sides, pinching and clutching. Larry's face had been more than Dave could bear to look at, and he had turned away with only the dead-weight sound of Larry's feet being dragged across the porch. A short few minutes later, the car's motor revved two quick times and then burst into a roar that faded slowly away.

Now the heat had hit a high point. The backyard and house were quiet. She was inside, Dave knew that, but also knew there was little reason to expect any help with his plans. He had thought Clara might be helpful at first, but the reality was clear now. He pushed himself up and felt some of his old strength return. Stronger, feeling better, he pushed against the side of the shed and watched it saw and buckle with his weight. Immediately afterwards he dropped to his knees and jammed his eye to the door handle hole. Nothing. No movement from the house. He pushed again, dropped again, and this time saw Clara walk to a window of the house.

She was a big woman, not like Joe. It was plain that Larry inherited his size from his mother and her side of the family. Joe and his parents and grandparents, who had owned and worked this same poor land before him, were small people, short and skinny, but fierce and left alone due to a combination of meanness and meanness on top of that. Clara stood framed in the window. She leaned over and pressed her hands against the window, her features somehow dropped onto her face, sagging, unflinching.

Dave took the two good-sized steps back the shed would allow for and hit a spot on the wall. When he did, his knee popped through the hole he pulled loose from the bottom half of the wall. He had forgotten about the hole he pulled loose from the rotted boards earlier that morning. Without returning to the knob hole to check on Clara, he started pulling again at the boards just to the right and left of the palm-sized hole. Small but inspiring splinters of dark wood had just started to peel away between his sore fingertips when he heard the back door open and slam shut.

Through his two inch by two inch view of the outside world, Dave saw Clara drop heavily down the steps leading off the back porch. She stopped at the base of the steps and squatted slowly to pluck at two or three dust-powdered flowers sprouting from sheer will out of the dreary,   grassless earth forming a radius along the edge of the house. She pushed them with the tops of her fingernails very gently and then pulled at them, attempting, it seemed, to straighten the weak and failing stems. She did this for nearly a full minute and then walked the short distance across to the dog house.

She bent awkwardly to the ground, glared into the opening of the tiny dog house, and rested her hand across the top of the tin roof. Instantly she pulled her hand away. The tin was already scorched to a stove-top sear. When she did turn her attention to where Dave struggled to keep sight of her through the knob hole, she grew excited and moved swiftly to the door of the shack. She made no sound as she approached the door and Dave heard the rattle of the cooking pan bouncing against rocks and dirt as she picked it from the ground. She stalked off to the edge of the house and suddenly stopped. It was then Dave noticed the small well. She pulled the rope and a bucket slithered into her hands. She pulled the pan from where she tucked it under her arm and dipped it into the water. The sunlight reflected off the water and Dave could make out the way it moved and lifted inside the pan. Cold and wet. It reminded him of his thirst and how he should probably be dead, according to his great-grandmother and her one day rule.

Remembering this, Dave felt the energy he had discovered and harnessed earlier pour from him in defeated waves. The simple act of keeping his head held upright long enough to look through the hole became more than he could manage.

It seemed that several minutes passed in the half-dark when the door tore open and a sunburst of light blinded him. It took a moment, but when his eyes adjusted he saw Clara looming above him holding the dull baking pan with water sloshing back and forth and spilling from the edges. The water landed in large swelled drops and then scattered across the dust, splashing onto the ground and then forming small mud pellets at her feet.

"Com' on." She grabbed the top of his arm hard, digging her fingers into the muscles there. "Take a drink of this, now. Drink this."

She pushed the lip of the pan to his mouth and tilted it. Water ran over his face and he cracked open his mouth. The feeling was better than anything he had ever experienced. The skin along his back broke out in goosebumps shivered as the water dumped down his throat. Before long he was gulping and then, in one instant motion, he vomited it back up, over his teeth and onto the ground. It cascaded from his mouth in a fierce spray. Some of it coated the tops of Clara's feet.

She returned to the well and brought another pan full of water and he drank. This time was able to keep it down. It was cold in his stomach and for the first time since it had started last night, there was no dry click when he breathed. The sound had been something he had gotten used to and now it was gone.

He was rubbing his lips and eyeing the pan when she grabbed his arm again, pulling him to his feet. He swayed against the wall and bumped his knee. He was reminded of the hole he had been trying to tear loose and instinctively moved to cover it with his hands.

She saw him try to hide evidence of his progress and shook her head, clearly disappointed. "Honey, that don't matter right now. Don't you know that? Right now we're goin' in the house. Me and you are about to have some big fun."

23

"I didn't stay gone for too long, though," John Harper said.

They had moved onto the front porch after Harper's quiet wife moved with her beans to the kitchen.

"I went back home. I was running down the road like crazy. Call the cops, call the police. That was all that was going through my mind." He stuck an oak splinter into his teeth and leaned back in his chair. "But I was scared. Plain and simple. I was scared. Larry had got hurt on my property, and I guess I don't have to tell you that having a dozen or so cops out on my property was something I wasn't real keen on seeing happen." He stopped and dropped his head, unable to return his gaze to Paul.

"Why'd you go back?"

"I had to do something."

"What'd you do?"

Things went silent for awhile with just the rocking of the chairs the only sound along the ridge. Harper only looked out into his yard. There was nothing out there but a couple of birds jumping around in a puddle of water, but he looked anyway. He studied them, the two birds, for a long time.

"I just went back," he said finally. "I got there real late at night. It might have been real early in the morning. I know that because I figured it would be safer to walk back that way with nobody around. When I got there everything was quiet, so I went up to the window and looked in. It was the living room, must have been, and nobody was in there. So I went to the other window and saw Larry lying on the bed in there. He was covered up and I could see him shivering in the bed. He had his eyes open just laying there and shivering. It was terrible."

"Where was my dad?"

"I didn't know right away, so I just went up on the hillside there behind the house and watched for some time. Then when it started getting that real dull light like right before sunrise, I saw Joe Fenner come out on the porch."

Harper continued to talk and as he did, Paul began to feel sick. It was the story, the words. It was the way his face looked, the tone of his voice. It felt like guilt to Paul, and it felt like hell, he was sure.

"I watched through a window after Joe and Larry left for as long as I could stand it, but it wasn't something I wanted to keep watching. It was as wrong as anything I'd ever seen before or since."

Paul asked anyway, wanted to know. Had to know.

"It was your daddy and Joe's wife. Jesus, Paul. They were in there together in Larry's room on that bed

166

with the covers in the floor. There was blood all over the covers and in the floor and they were on that bed, Paul. Do I have to keep talking about this? Can't you figure it out? Can't you mostly figure it out without having to hear it?"

But Paul needed to hear it. He pushed and pushed until Harper was sitting bolt upright in his chair, clenching his hands together, talking with a heaviness Paul had never heard before in another's man's voice. He spat the words out at Paul. At once he seemed disgusted to be articulating the words and then happy to be purging them from his body, one syllable at a time. When he was finished, he dropped back into his chair, drained and empty.

Paul thought for awhile before saying, "And then you went back home and he stayed there for two more days?" He was trying to sound quizzical and leave it at that, but the anger was coming through and there was little he could do to control himself. "That's good Mr. Harper. That's real good."

"Paul, you have to understand--"

"Do I? Why's that, exactly? I get that part about you being scared of your own shadow. I get the part about being afraid to deal with people, but you could have just called the cops, told them where Dad was and not gave a name."

Harper tore his gaze from the floor, where he had kept it fixed and rigid for several minutes, and looked directly at Paul.

"You think I haven't had that on my mind for all

these years?" Harper said. "You think I don't know the things I could've done? What I'm telling you, the only thing I can tell you, is what I did. You see? It don't matter what could have been. If a bullfrog had wings, it wouldn't bump its ass all the time. All I can tell you is *what I did*."

Paul didn't speak, didn't nod, didn't move an inch in his chair. If a bullfrog had wings. If a bullfrog had wings. The words crawled over Paul's body like fire.

"I told you before about things settling," Harper said. "How I told you about some places just not fit for settling when I first saw you. You remember that? Well, that's what I've been trying to do ever since that summer. Just workin' to settle, and it can't be done, not really. I found some peace here, but what happened to your daddy is
something I ain't never told another living soul. Not even him. He never named it, and so I left it right there too. My Augustine ain't heard all of it. You're the only one."

Paul stood and let the chair tilt back and bang against the side of the house. The sudden movement startled Harper and he grabbed the sides of his own chair and looked up into the doorway. His wife was standing there with her arms hanging lifelessly to her sides, her face entirely blank.

Paul turned to look at her and then put his hand through his hair and pushed air between his lips, letting it whistle through and escape in a rush, bottled up but now released. Without a handshake for Harper or a word to his wife, Paul started off the porch but the woman asked him to stop, to wait. Turning, he was still surprised to be face to face with Harper's wife. She was much taller than he realized, and her features brought to mind old family photographs full of grim and serious people that fill attics and basements. She spoke again, and, when she spoke, the words were dry, as if they had been lodged in her throat for years and years.

"There's gonna be a day," she said, "and it'll feel like tomorrow, when you'll be over this and done with it." She stopped, looked back at Harper, and turned back to Paul. "But it's not going to be today."

24

Dave didn't so much sit on the couch as try to melt into it. If he could sink far enough, down into the dust and mold, he could get away, he thought. His stomach ached again from drinking the water too fast and to counter the feeling he tried to sit as still as possible. He kept himself bent slightly to the left, the same position she left him in after pulling him through the kitchen and past a small hallway. He had gotten a look at himself in a stand-up mirror in the middle of the hallway as she dragged him to the living room. He tried to forget how he had looked in the mirror. Instead he waited and listened to her moving around in what must have been her bedroom. But he couldn't forget. He knew now that his eyes looked like sunken black pits, knotholes like the ones he dug sap from the pines up at White Mountain. While passing the mirror, he had seen a crow's nest of black, matted hair jumping in a series of feathered tornados off the top and sides of his head.

"Little Shannon ain't so little these days, huh." Clara stood in the doorway. When Dave saw her he immediately began holding his breath and sat bolt upright on the couch. For the first time in hours he wasn't thinking about water.

Clara had changed clothes. She now wore what looked to Dave like a thin white dress, much shorter than the dress she had been wearing. It moved like silk across the humps of her stomach and hips, slid easily across the expanse of her upper thighs. She smiled, revealing teeth that were split and gashed and ragged, and pushed fallen strands of hair from her forehead.

He wasn't thinking about water, exactly, but food was there. Hot food, warm and rich in flavor, biscuits and gravy, pork chops and buttered mashed potatoes. Water could wash it down, but even with Clara standing in the doorway, one arm stretched to the ceiling to hold to the top of the paint-chipped door, the other on her wide hip, it was food that Dave hoped for.

"Can I have something to eat?"

This seemed to please Clara instantly and the smile grew wide. More teeth, less teeth, bashed, crooked. Her arm came down and landed firmly on her other hip. She tilted her head sideways and her face became serious. She started walking across to him, slowly at first, and then faster across the hardwood floor in her bare feet.

"Can I have something to eat?" He asked again after she sat down beside him on the small couch. She rubbed her leg against his. "Can I go home?"he whispered. He felt tears building in the corners of his eyes.

"No, you can't go home. But you *can* have something to eat."

Dave's instincts were to look away as Clara raised her slip up across her kneecaps. He turned his head and she grabbed it in both her hands and snapped it back around, pulling his head downward, closer to her thighs. She tugged again at the slip and it popped above her hips. Beneath were two wide thighs, white and flabby, hairs sprouting here and there from moles and various spots. And in the middle of his field of vision was something he had seen many times in magazines, but never in real life. A large patch of coarse brown hair about the size of an adult's fist stood out like a brown boat amid the white caps of her thighs.

"You know what to do with something like that?" She said, tossing her hair down from its fixings so that it spilled across her back. She leaned back on the couch now, her legs splayed outward. Her left foot was tucked into the cushions along the back of the couch, taking hold, causing the muscles in her legs to jump while she balanced. Dave was afraid to move his eyes. When he offered no movement or comment, Clara pulled the slip over her head in one fluid motion and, in an instant, was completely naked, stretching her back across the couch arm so that David could see the slightest hint of ribs poking out from beneath the huge double mass that was her breasts. He had never seen breasts that large in magazines before. And, despite his hunger and the pain still stinging through his body, and regardless of how appalling she was to look at flopped across the couch the way she was, he felt himself stir. He had explored with a couple of girls, but never this close. He felt himself stir again and it made him sick. He leaned forward and vomited into the floor.

"Jesus!" She thrashed on the couch, flesh moving, bare feet beating against the floor as she leaned over. "Look what you did, you little shit!"

Nothing was real. Things were filtered through a haze of vomit and pain and confusion. He only felt a rough tug when she took a handful of his hair and jerked his head back. Something snapped when she did, just below the nape of his neck and everything was stiff. Her foot slid through the vomit on the floor.

"We'll take care of that later," she said. Her voice was a hiss, a furnace ready to blow. She still had Dave's hair pinched through a fist of tight fingers. "Now eat!"

Suffocating. Gagging. Everything in his body revolted and went clam, revolted again and went calm. He concentrated on other things, any other things he could get himself to think of while trying not to listen to her instructions. Left, right, up, down. He could hardly hear, his face and neck buried into the patch of brown, his hands clasped firmly against the white ocean thighs pumping his shoulders up and down with movement he could not have managed on his own.

It was almost dark when she finally finished with him. They had moved to the bedroom by that time and she had left him scattered across the bed and disappeared into the hallway. She returned some minutes later wearing a different dress than she had on before. Her hair was placed back into a bun on the back of her head. She looked exactly the same as when she had came to the shed some hours ago, only now her face was flushed red, her lips chapped and cracked from breathing heavily for so long.

"Come on. Let's get you back out there."

Her steps were light and she moved swiftly across the bedroom. Giddy, that's what Dave would think later, when he understood some of the things that could get a person's spirits up that quickly. At the side of the bed, she took his arm firmly in her hand and pulled him up. His clothes were dirty and smelled bad, crumpled in a blood stained wad at the side of the bed. She picked them up with her other hand and tossed them in his lap.

"You can put them back on when we get out there. Ain't nobody gonna see you trotting across the yard." She paused, smiled, ran a hand across her hair, touched her flushed red cheek. "Ain't nobody but me gonna see that pretty little backside."

She waited for him to stand and then smacked him once across the ass. Dave dropped his head and tried to cover himself with his free hand. His clothes — socks, underwear, shirt and pants — were tucked beneath his arm.

On the way back to the shed, she watched the hills closely and ran her fingers down his spine, a light touch, all the way to the top of his ass, where she brushed gently with two fingers. When they made it to the door of the shed, she turned him around, pushed herself close to him and grabbed him in her hand. He kept his head lowered and didn't look up. He closed his eyes hard while she moved her hand, slowly at first, and then faster until he started getting hard, growing in her fist.

"See there, you little shit. You liked it all along." Then, still stroking him, she leaned in close and put a finger under his chin. He looked up into her eyes, which were soft and seemed to be someplace else. "You breathe a word and you know he'll kill you, don't you? You know better to say anything, cause he'll kill you and make it hurt. See, I know that's what you're thinking, he'll kill me anyway, but not like that he wouldn't. You see, this'll be me and your little secret, huh. Little secret. You tell him, he'll skin you like one of 'em old hogs out there. We'll eat you up just like one of 'em so nobody ever finds anything. We'll grind the bones up and dust 'em across that piss poor field out there."

Dave was getting sick again. He was so hard inside her fast moving fist it was starting to hurt too. And then he went, he wasn't sure if it would happen. He had done it several times himself, but he was always thinking about good things. This time, he just went, the same way he might have coughed if he'd had a cold. A physical reaction to something that was happening to his body.

She was smiling now, and laughing. She raised her hand to her face and looked at it in the fading light. It glistened and sparkled as she moved her hand closer to her face. Dave vomited again when she sniffed it and then touched her tongue gently to the palm of her hand.

"We are going to have so much fun, me and you. You just wait and see, little Shannon." She wiggled her shoulders. "My little Shannon."

The door closed slowly bringing the darkness spiked with purple rays of twilight through the loose boards of the shed. Dave scrambled across the dirt floor, moving his hands in large sweeping motions through his own vomit and found his clothes.

Outside the shed he could hear whistling. Through the hole in the door he could see Clara. She was plucking absently at the flowers at the foot of the steps leading up to the porch. Dave looked at her dress, hanging about a foot below her knees, thought about her legs and vomited again, white and yellow bile across his lap, his empty stomach cramping as he finished.

They fed him very little over the next two days before a police officer knocked on the door and asked if they'd seen David Shannon, William Shannon's boy. It was slop, meant mostly for the hogs, and he did good to eat it without losing it back up again. He lived, he figured later, on the two Mason jars of green beans he found on the last morning he was in the shed. He noticed them along the top shelf and brought them down with his heart ramming against anything near it. He ate more than half of the first jar before screwing the copper-colored lid back on. A short time later, he unscrewed it, took two more beans and a large drink of the water sloshing around inside, and replaced the lid. He put both jars back in their spot. Joe hadn't came back into the shed for tools or anything of that nature, but he didn't want to take the chance that mean old Joe would find his hidden life line. He had been thinking a lot about death in the hours leading up to discovering the jars of beans, and now, for the first time since he had been taken prisoner, he was thinking about life.

Larry was back home, having spent a day in the hospital undergoing emergency surgery for his left hip and two badly pulverized legs. The details were lost on Dave. He heard Joe and Clara talking on the porch the evening Larry was brought home; he remembered hearing that word *pulverized* and feeling what it meant. He remembered Larry pancake flat against the pile of coal like a yellowed toenail at the base of the tipple. It was amazing that he was home at all.

But not having him home was not acceptable. Joe made that clear, and no one questioned it. Larry was home, huddled in the back room dealing with his pain while Dave dealt with his in the shed.

It was early afternoon by the time the first cop knocked on the front door of the Fenner's home. Dave was sleeping, taking advantage of an uncommonly cool afternoon that gave back his lungs, beaten from heat and exposure to little or no clean air.

Larry heard them from his bedroom, talking to his mother and father. His eyes searched the ceiling, jerked left to right while he listened.

That's a shame, officer.

Don't they have an idea where he'd be?

When did they see him last?

Larry shook his head and his eyes and his arms. He would have jerked his legs if he could have moved them.

They say he was with our boy the last time anybody saw him? Who said that?

Well it matters to us, I reckon.

The sound of the cop's cruiser engine revving in the driveway woke Dave up and he just had a chance to see through the hole the blue and white car with the large antenna rolling back and away from the Fenner house. He couldn't help himself and at the risk of attracting attention after such a long break, he banged his fist against the door and started to cry.

He was still crying when Joe slammed the back door and stomped down the front steps. The shed door popped open on its hinges. Dave noticed above Joe's head the dull gray sky. Summer rain.

He looked down on Dave. "Sonofabitch." He put his hands on his hips and spit sideways and cocked his head. "Come on! Sonofabitch."

Dave didn't move. He thought about standing, but then decided to sit and wait to see what Joe wanted. His heart was racing. He felt like he would pass out. Joe grabbed him by the arm and pulled him to a standing position. He could see most of the boy's ribs when he got him standing. Served him right, busting up his boy's legs like that and then showing up here like he did. And even if he hadn't busted up Larry's legs, sometimes little pricks like Dave Shannon just needed to be reminded of a few things. He liked to be the one reminding. But that was over now. Fucking cops. Somebody told about what happened out at the tipple. All he knew was that Larry fell off the tipple. That's what Larry had told him. He figured out himself that it was Dave's fault. That part wasn't hard. What had him thinking was who it was that reported this little skinny shit missing so quick. It was probably one of those other boys always running with Dave and his brother. It sure as shit wasn't William Shannon. The man was at work too much to notice. The boy's mother would have just thought he was off staying with somebody. That's what he had relied on. But now this.

The cop that came knocking was a boy Joe recognized, and he heard while getting gas at Cramer's that the Shannons had reported Dave missing the evening after he didn't come home after school. He overheard someone say they read an article about the missing Shannon boy is the newspaper. The Shannons must have called them, asked them to put a missing person's notice in or something. Chip Evers must have needed something to write about and wrote a whole hellfire story on the little prick. Three days and already he was *the missing Shannon boy*. But Joe had a plan now. To make it work would take some doing, planning that started now, here in the doorway of the shed.

Joe stepped into the shed but then reeled

backward and covered his mouth and nose with the palm of his hand. The boy had used the bathroom in one corner and it smelled far worse than even the pig lot. He crossed the shed and took Dave's arm.

"You bout to go," he said. "I'm gonna take you out to the tracks on Elm Branch and gonna let you out. I'm gonna call the goddam newspaper first and tell them I saw that *missing fucking Shannon boy* out there on the tracks on Elm Branch." He stopped at once, pulled Dave to his feet. "You gettin' this? You'll want to remember everything from now until you get back home real clear, cause it's real important. If word gets out about what's happened here, about you being here, I don't think I need to tell you what will happen."

Dave's arm hurt. Everything in the past few days had been converted to physical reactions of pain and hunger. He understood what Joe had told him, but his main concern was for the two jars of green beans on the shelf. He was sure Joe was going to notice them and break them and laugh and leave, even though he only stared down on Dave. If he turned his head just an inch or two he'd see the jars. Though he understood what Joe had said, he wasn't convinced any of it was real or true.

"You better understand me, boy," Joe said and jumped into Dave's face, his nose so close to Dave's face that he could see three long hairs crawling from the left nostril toward his slightly crooked upper lip. "I'm lettin' you go." Joe stopped, stood as if thinking about this statement and the weight it carried and then leaned back into Dave's face. "But what I probably ought to do is kill you."

Joe stood and scratched his chin a moment, thinking about how he could do it. He could do it and never get caught, that was sure. But the police had already visited his house. Had they visited other houses in the area? Had someone saw the little shit here at his house and reported it and the cops were just playing dumb, luring him in, keeping watch. No, he couldn't kill him, he figured. No matter how nice that would be.

"Naw, I guess I can't kill you. But that's what I'd do if I knew I could. Let's go."

He didn't see the beans, Dave thought as Joe jerked him by the elbow out of the shed. He's not going to take the beans, the magic beans. "The magic beans."

"Huh? What'd you say?"

When Dave didn't answer, Joe turned fast with the nose hairs and heavy breathing. "Look at me. Look at me!"

Dave pulled his gaze from the ground. The beans were gone for good now. No way around it. When he looked up, he saw Joe's elbow bending back and then his fist coming fast at his face and there was nothing he could do about it.

"Right there you go, you horrible little cripplin' fuck!" Joe slammed his fist a second time into Dave's mouth and smiled at the pain he felt in his knuckles as they smacked across and against Dave's teeth and lips. The lip was split almost in half with the first punch and the second sent a tooth down Dave's throat. Dave gagged on it and dropped to the ground, his mouth transformed into a faucet of dark red-black blood. And Joe dropped to his knees in front of the boy, swiveled his head left and right, checked the surrounding hills, making sure no squirrel hunters or anybody else was perched on a nearby ridge, and then pushed the ball of his elbow up into Dave's face once, twice, sending him flailing backward onto his back.

"Now, now, now," Joe panted. His chest was heaving up and down and he couldn't keep his arms still; his fists wanted more action. What a spectacle he must have been if someone had seen him spinning in the yard with arms out of control over Dave Shannon on the ground, a bloody mess full of crying and bleeding.

Kill him.

It sounded good. The problems with that simple plan that had been running through his head earlier were gone now, tucked neatly aside by adrenaline and power and rage, his interchangeable constants.

"That shed's nice and comfy ain't it, boy? I done my time in that shit hole, same as Larry, same as you, and done it hard. But your time's done now." He leaned in closer, his cheekbone brushing Dave's busted nose he was so close. "Yes, yes, yes. I think I am gonna kill you, prick." He jumped up and slung his arms in the air and twirled around. When he leaned back over, pressing in close to Dave again, he was a god and yelled into the boy's face thunder and lightning and hail.

Dave cut the yell in half, all elbows and pushing and thrusts, and then Joe was reduced from his god-self to an old man again, gurgling on blood and drowning from a hole in his throat about the size of a quarter. Dave dropped the blunt stick, now covered in warm blood, to his side. He had shoved it into the side of Joe Fenner's neck without a thought. There had been a thick suction when he pulled it loose. Exhausted, Dave relaxed his head onto the ground and, beyond his control, fell immediately into a drained, steady sleep.

In the car it was silence he remembered most, and the back of Clara's head, shaking and moving back and forth from side to side. The whispers and the hissing he would remember later in his dreams and in the fields overseas. It was the sound of the rain coming across the rice field that brought the hisses back to his memory then, just before the full storm hit across his platoon, young men huddled together and tired of the rain, tired of the fear. This hiss, when the coming rain was still just a distant sound beating a millions dents across the field, was the sound Clara Fenner kept making while she drove him out to Elm Branch. It was the sound she spat into his face as she dropped him from the car and onto the tracks. And it was the sound the car made as it disappeared and became part of the terrible past.

25

Paul hitchhiked back to Red Knife. The trip was dark and cold. The man who gave him a ride wasn't a talker. He mentioned he drove a coal truck, spent about three minutes complaining that all his co-workers stayed high on nerve pills and speed, and then went quiet. Some kind of miracle for sure, Paul figured, that anyone would pick up a hitchhiker these days. But, hitchhiking or not, Red Knife was a dangerous place. Dangerous now; dangerous when his dad was growing up. Paul thought of all that John Harper told him, how he would have never imagined that Larry's family, his parents, were that demented. It was one thing to know that people had meanness in their hearts, but it was another thing entirely to imagine the type of meanness leading them to the kind of acts John had described.

From the moment he left John Harper's house he had felt listless in a way he would never feel again, untethered and spirit-starved. If a mind could truly overflow, this would be that time for Paul. Overflowing, maybe, but not a single thought among it all about his father. He had spent nearly his entire life either openly hating his father or secretly hating him, down so deep inside his secret self even he couldn't realize how dark the impressions ran. What he felt now, though, was a cream-colored void, no passion to speak of good or bad. His father experienced something terrible and it changed his life. But the thing for Paul was simply this: it changed his life too. This fact blending with the new facts of his father's past had placed Paul into a kind of mental lockdown. Watching the guardrail from the passenger window, his only thought was sleep.

When he got to his grandparents' house he stumbled through the kitchen. He passed the guest bedroom and navigated the living room and went into his father's old bedroom. He stepped into the bedroom and, without turning on the light, peeled his shirt off and slid his shoes off at the foot of the bed.

The room was full of ghosts and fears. It was candy apple-dipped in mental darkness. Paul could make out the silhouette of the bed and pushed ahead until his knee bumped its corner. He then turned sideways and sat down heavily. What else might be waiting for him under the mattress? The bed springs pinched and jabbed his back, prodded him to lift it like a cellar door and fumble for other artifacts, puzzle pieces. But as his eyes adjusted to the dark, the pictures on the walls, pictures of him, became his focus. He was hidden there. He was the next artifact. He alone remained unturned.

He came awake slowly, turning on his side. The springs still snagged and scraped his ribs, but it was the smell of his father that brought him completely awake.

The room was slightly lighter. It must have been early morning. He could make out things now, and he felt rested. He closed his eyes again and breathed into the pillow. His breath raised the smell of his father again, and again he opened his eyes.

The first thing he saw when he opened his eyes this time was the Mason jar of money sitting on the nightstand. The crumpled bills outlined by shadows. He reached across the bed and took the jar in his hand. He brought it close to his face. The lid was old and rusted. He turned it over in both hands, now lying on his back. With a quick flick of his wrist he spun the lid loose and pulled it off. He turned sideways on the bed and dumped the contents on the mattress. Coins scattered inside dark ridges of tossed sheets. The bills tumbled across the bed, along with the letter. He flicked the letter with his fingernail and then looked to the green bills. He picked a handful up and stuffed them in the jar, holding it closer to the growing light coming through the window. He lay like that for a long time while morning broke making the green of the dollar bills more and more visible through the jar. After a long while of this, he got out of bed, dressed in a rush and snatched the keys to the car as he left the house. He had a better than average idea of where the house was, but the overgrown dirt road was so infrequently traveled he might as well have been driving along the side of a hill. He clutched the steering wheel and braced as the windshield of the car tore at and took hits from sagging tree branches that had stretched and then dropped across the road.

It was just past eight when he came to a rolling stop in front of the old Fenner home. Beside him, the Mason jar rolled back and forth in the passenger seat, empty now.

It was smaller than Paul had imagined. A rectangle of matted leaves and bald spots showing dirt made up the front yard. This had been the garden. Around the spot where the garden had been were the remnants of a knotted wooden fence. Once well-constructed, what was left of the fence lay in ruins, mostly rotted and falling apart.

The house looked much the same. Probably in poorer condition than when his father was younger, the house was now a brown and moss green patchwork blending into the trees and bushes that had either crawled up its sides or clutched onto the roof, which Paul noticed was partly collapsed. On the dilapidated front porch was a single wooden chair. Paul stared at it for a long time before getting out of the car. There he could feel a ghost, or a spirit, a demon. All real and all whole and into the world, but also nothing, only an empty rocking chair.

He slammed the car door shut and checked his back pocket for his father's letter. He had taken the money, folded it into his wallet. The change he dropped into a cup on the kitchen table. Satisfied that the letter was still in his pocket he walked into the overgrown leaves, turning the jar in his hands as he went.

Connected to the far end of the house was what Paul considered a simple carport, but what he figured must have been where Joe Fenner kept his horses. Two thick posts stuck up from the ground under the shed like rotten teeth. The ground beneath the covering was trampled and sported large ridges. He navigated along these ridges to the back of the house and came to the porch.

The yard in back was a carbon copy of the front, with the only exception being the absence of the rectangular ghost of a garden, and, of course, the tool shed. The tool shed remained. About fifteen feet from the back porch it stood at half attention. Although still standing, it now tilted to the left. A stiff push would send it to the ground. Scattered around the shed and back porch were an assortment of tools, rusted and broken. A garden tiller and, not far away, a skeletal set of mattress springs, presumably used to drag the garden. The back door of the house stood open, hanging by a single hinge.

Paul started for the door and stopped. He turned the jar over in his hands and then turned again and started to the shed. He stuck his index finger through the hole in the door and gently tugged. The door cracked open about three inches and then stopped, stuck in high grass. Paul shifted the tables of grass with the tip of his shoe and gave a firm jerk. The door broke off and pulled his arm, gravity heavy, to the ground. He regained his footing and dropped the door into the grass and stepped inside the shed.

In the five or six seconds it took for his eyes to adjust all Paul was left with was the slightly cool breeze coming from inside the shed and the scent of earth and old wood. As the corners of the shed's insides started coming into the view, the first thing he noticed was a brown, rusted gasoline can ahead of him against the far wall. To the left was the bent section of wall that caused the tilt. Paul kicked lightly near the bottom at a small hole there, a place where the wood had given way to leave an opening, tugged at by animals, maybe. To the right, he immediately saw the cuts in the wood. Deep scratches roughly two inches long. They covered the wall. Paul held his hand up and ran his finger along one of the slashes, felt where the wood had peeled away in a ribbon. They started at about his eye level and extended down the wall to about his knees. He bent and brushed a fingerprint along the marks nearest the bottom. These were smaller, about a half inch each, and not as deeply cut. Some had nearly faded away, nothing more than frantic whispers of scratches.

Above the gas can was what had once served as a bench. Where it once was fixed to the wall it now hung limply downward, held by two rusted nails at each end. Above this was a shelf that had held better over time. Along the shelf were three Mason jars. There was a space for one more on the end. He held his jar up and examined the rusted top again. He very delicately placed it beside the others and then stood back.

He hadn't planned to do this, but the opportunity was there, had presented itself as if sent from somewhere divine by someone divine. The jar was where some almighty wanted it to be. At that moment, the moment when Paul was admiring his own unique thoughtfulness, there came the distinct breaking of dry leaves and branches being cracked and broken behind him. All at once the doorway of the shed filled with a large, silhouetted figure. It was all he had time to determine and then something connected with the side of his head and there was only the dirt floor and the fog and then nothing.

In the abyss of his unconscious it was his father again, floating in the black holding cold slabs of chalk and broken bottles.

The first thing Paul realized was the unbelievable pain in his head. The second thing he noticed was that he couldn't reach his hand to examine where the pain was coming from. His arms were pinned to his sides. Stretched out on a bed, his arms and legs had been tied to the mattress. The straps seemed to be leather and apparently ran under the bed, latched together somewhere beneath him. There was a window at his feet. Outside, two birds sat idly along the window sill. They pecked at the cuticle-soft wood and flew away. Just like that.

Larry Fenner sat in a chair across the room. He was slumped in the chair, his body limp and relaxed.

His head was tilted down so that his chin lay on his chest. Paul couldn't tell if he was crying or grinning. He lifted his head and stared at Paul with electric eyes that jittered in their sockets. Paul heard a scratching sound and saw that Larry was pulling his fingernails across the arms of the chair. They twitched with the same quickness as did his eyes. A delicate rope of spit hung from his peeled back lips, dropped and hung there briefly before snapping in half. Larry licked his bottom lip.

"Paul Shannon," he said. His voice was low, full of baritone again and hatred.

Paul tossed his head back onto the pillow. He could still see Larry from the corner of his eye and tried to conceal his panic when Larry stood up.

"Paul Shaaaaaaaaaannon," Larry said again.

There was no reason not to face him. Whatever insanity this was, it was going to keep moving forward, so Paul stopped looking at the ceiling, turned his head, and watched Larry cross the room.

The dress Larry wore was a pale yellow, flower print. The thin fabric hung from his shoulders, lost in folds of thick muscle. He was barefoot and the dress stopped at his kneecaps. Paul could see the tangled and scarred mess that covered Larry's shins and ankles as he moved across the room. He dragged behind him with a single finger a large cane. The cane scraped across the hardwood. Once he was across the room, Larry swept his hand across the top of a mahogany dresser and came away with a pistol.

"Jesus, Larry. Jesus Christ, Larry."

Paul broke over. The panic he had been able to keep under control didn't waver. It didn't become shaky. That panic broke perfectly in two like a tree bent in a thunderstorm, bent until it snaps fully through. He writhed against the straps and buried his head far down into the pillow. He arched his back and pushed his legs out but then went still on the bed. If anything, the straps had tightened around his chest and legs.

Larry stalked back to the chair and plopped down, laying the pistol across his thigh, the cane now clutched in his left hand. He rapped it against the floor five times, muttered something Paul couldn't make out, and then stood up. The gun clattered to the floor. Larry had the cane in both hands now and in seconds was standing over Paul.

"What're you doing? Larry?"

Larry raised the cane above his head and then brought it down hard across Paul's legs. Paul heard a snapping sound with the first hit and then nothing above his own screams on the second and third hit. Then Larry stopped and let the cane fall from his grasp. It lopped against the bed and then rolled off to the floor. Without a sound he ignored Paul's open sobbing and staggered back to the chair. He bent and plucked the pistol from the floor and returned it to his thigh. His head dropped again, his chin pointed down, his eyes were fixed on Paul but hectic.

Paul could only look back. He was crying hard now. His head and legs throbbed in painful rhythm with his heartbeat, clubbing against his ribs.

"Have a look here, Paul Shannon." Larry's voice was different, a higher pitch, a straining squeak. He leered at Paul and gently tugged at the dress. It rose slowly across the tops of his terrible knees until he was exposed naked beneath. Clumsily, and with absent regard, he took himself and began masturbating half-heartedly, tossing himself back and forth. "We can have a good time, Paul Shannon. It's okay."

"Oh God, oh God," Paul held his breath and squeezed his eyes shut. The world had ended. This was how his time in this world ended. And there, at the end of the world, Larry stopped pulling at himself and took the gun from his leg. He staggered to his feet in such a way that the dress fell back into place, stopping with a swish against his hairless white legs. He had the gun at his side for one, two seconds before pointing it at Paul's head. When Paul didn't look, he pushed the end of the barrel against one eyelid. The eyeball sunk painfully far back into the socket.

Paul stopped moving against the straps. He lay still in the bed and watched images behind his eyelids. Images mostly of his father, but some were of his mother. His poor mother. His mommy. These images were smoke and dotted here and there with a set of kind brown eyes. The eyes seemed to look down on him from somewhere above him and he could tell by the way the creases around the eyes bunched at the skin that she was smiling. His mommy. It was everything he could do not to call out for her now, about to die here inside the boogeyman's cave.

Focusing on his mom had almost worked, but Paul could still hear Larry breathing hard. He felt the cold circle of the gun barrel leave his eyelid, the weight from it leaving a ghost of an indention and pressure there. And he opened his eyes. When he did, he saw Larry bring the gun slowly up the side of his own head. The image was so unexpected that Paul's senses all but shut down. There were words still left within the spinning of his consciousness, words like birds chattering.

There's gonna be a day.

Sounds like glass shattering.

And it'll feel like tomorrow.

His eyes wide open now, he watched. Larry lowered the pistol as if he might have come to his senses, forgotten the years of abuse and watching abuse, lying about it, making up stories to explain abuse. Larry stretched out a smile, a fake smile more unholy and unnatural than any mask, any demon or fiery archangel. In one clean motion he changed the position of the pistol again to press the end of the barrel into his own neck. It seemed he rushed to do it before his next thought made its way through the calamity of all his days before this one. With a hard jerk Larry pulled the trigger, and only then did his unnatural smile disappear in the tumbling folds of his lips.

26

There was nothing after Larry shot himself. Not really. Only blood and hours of twisting on the bed until he worked his leg loose enough to free the rest of himself. And then after that, more twisting, this time with various narratives for law enforcement followed by his refusing a trip in the ambulance. Larry had pounded his legs with his cane, but nothing that seemed to have broken any bones. The police were mostly half-hearted in with their questions: How did he end up here? What was his connection to Larry Fenner? Series after series of the same questions asked in different ways. None of it at all interesting to Paul. His total and absolute attention was now focused on the letter in his back pocket. The letter his dad stuffed inside a Mason jar during some lonely moment amid an ocean of lonely moments.

Paul sat down on his father's old bed to read another line of the letter which had accompanied the two-hundred and some odd dollars inside the jar. He heard loose springs rattle against one another with metal friction when he relaxed down into a six-foot long groove pressed, over the years, along the right side of the bed. When he settled on the bed, pill bottles rolled against his back. Paul grabbed some of the empty bottles that were darkened by age — Marplan and Nardil — and reached behind him until he found bottles with pills still in them — Effexor, Zoloft, Serzone, Topamax. He gathered the bottles and placed each one carefully along the night stand beside the bed and then held the letter up to a small shaft of light coming from the room's single window.

The writing was scrawled and barely legible, probably would have been to the untrained eye. But Paul had been reading his father's letters for many years and knew the great swooping *h* and the jagged *r* as clearly as typed and formatted business correspondence, and then the rest, each jagged letter and nervous word. His father's nervous handwriting was replaced with gashing red green and black crayon marks, and then, below that, a stick-man with black hair holding a stick boy's three-fingered hand. Beneath the drawing Paul made while in grade school were his father's words, but he couldn't make them out. The letter was written over the drawing. Paul could see where the pen cut tiny paths through the crayon marks.

When he finished, Paul let the letter fall into his lap and lifted his legs slowly onto the bed. He stretched back and let his arms fall over his head. His eyes avoided the ceiling, and rested peacefully on his feet. Along the edges of his body, just like an embrace, the deep cast left in the bed from the years and decades his father spent in the exact same spot held him in place. In this spot, Paul allowed himself to imagine in full detail a life from this perspective, the hours that might pass with nothing more on his mind than a terrible series of days from his childhood so scarring he would never talk about it with anyone. David Shannon lived with that experience on the surface of his skin at all times.

But those thoughts, trying to put himself in that place, was eased when Paul remembered he was in a small bedroom in the back of his grandparents' house, protected and loved no matter what might come next. A newly formed womb away from the world. In this way, some of it made a strange sense. Solitude in this bedroom was a comfortable existence in its way, and final. Imagining himself safe and realizing this was the general state of mind his father likely was in during the last quarter century of his life, Paul's thoughts, for the first time in a long time, did not center on his father, but returned to his mom.

An evening at Ruby's, the restaurant where she worked nights. An old jukebox with songs like Chuck Berry's "My Ding-a Ling" and John Cougar Mellencamp's "Jack & Diane" played in rotation — the first for laughs and the second, he was sure, to help remind her that love could be waiting somewhere just as magical; standing with him in the IGA while he played with a toy she could never afford to buy, giving him those few minutes of fun while she pretended to choose between dry dog food or canned; changing wet bed sheets to get him in the dry one. More time in a bedroom like a miniature shipping crate with a single bed and a lamp standing crooked in the floor; hours and hours and hours filled with only him and her sharing their quiet and mutual sadness.

In every memory for all of his years his father had been a shade somewhere on the perimeter of these memories, a shadow as flighty as a dust mote in the corner of the eye and then gone. But now, lying in place of his father, consuming him in that way, it was only himself and his mom. Playing pepper passing baseballs in Lulie Bates trailer park, making Pillsbury cinnamon rolls on food stamps day, staying with aunts and uncles between apartments or homes rented in hollers all across Mays County. Her making that seem like part of an exciting, extended vacation.

Moving in seconds through these memories again, Paul was sure this nostalgia, the memories he secretly held to for survival his entire life, was not the kind of reality he had just endured at the hands of Larry Fenner, Larry who had once lived his own terrible life and was now flat on his back in the cold ground. Nostalgia could do nothing tangible to help him. His mom was no more real to him than his father had been, only opposites, the yin and yang of his inner mind. Life wasn't made up of good or bad experiences, only moments, one after the other after another in a steady march toward the unforgettably painful.

Paul settled more deeply into the cast left by his father's weight. The light in the room was almost yellow, serene. The lock on the door still worked fine. Very naturally, it occurred to him he could easily rest for a while in his father's old bed. William and Eve might tell a guest to move along after a couple days, but for blood they would, and did, offer an indefinite lifeline. He could stay here, take that lifeline, and look away from the world. So much would fall from concern, and, like his father, he would be alone but protected, sad but never in danger of becoming more sad, self-forsaken but set free from choice and consequence. He rolled onto his side, adjusted the pillow. A clock hand ticked from somewhere in the room and then blended into white noise. So many moments stopped in place, and all this time to spare.

Tomorrow he'd talk to his grandparents.

Tomorrow he'd stop planning what to do next.

Made in the USA
Columbia, SC
16 August 2020